BURDEN KANSAS

ALAN RYKER

Sucker Punch Press

Copyright © 2011 by Jeffrey Rice

This is a work of fiction. Any resemblance to actual persons, living
or dead, events, or locales is entirely coincidental.

Cover art "The Outsider That's Inside" by Justin Critch,
justin.critch@gmail.com, http://justincritch.daportfolio.com

Cover art "Bovine Skyline" by Nate Brelsford

Cover design by Wendy McBride, mcbride.wendy@gmail.com

Copy edit by Theresa D. Lininger, athenaedits@gmail.com,
http://athenaedits.com

ISBN: 061547537X
ISBN-13: 978-0615475370

Always to Christina.

CONTENTS

ACKNOWLEDGMENTS

Thanks to Christina and my entire family. Thanks to the artists I worked with: Wendy McBride, Justin Critch and Nate Brelsford. Thanks to my editor, Theresa Lininger. Thanks to Kirsten "Kiwi" Smith, who brainstormed with me to develop this story.

CHAPTER 1

Keith stood at his kitchen counter. He alternated between gulping down black coffee and taking bites out of a Hostess Fruit Pie. Out in the yard the dogs barked relentlessly. He ignored it for as long as he could but the sound bored into his head. Even though he wanted another fruit pie, he decided to check on the commotion.

The hot Kansas sun greeted him as he opened the door. The day would be scorching. The sun had bleached the color from the entire landscape. The fields. The outbuildings. The two-by-fours he'd used to build his big, wrap-around porch.

He stepped off the porch into his yard and walked around his white-slatted two-story house. His dogs bounced around and barked at a common center. They jumped in and out with their muzzles low. From the way they kept their distance, he knew what they barked at, but still he squinted until he saw it.

Keith went back to the house, reached in through the screen door and grabbed his shotgun. He walked across his lawn again.

"Back up."

The dogs didn't take their eyes off the rattler, but they backed up.

For a few seconds, Keith stared the creature in its eyes. It didn't look away. He had to respect that. He pulled the trigger and felt the familiar punch into his shoulder.

The snake's jaws opened and shut reflexively as Keith held it just behind the skull. He watched the rattler's fangs flex, as if nothing would satisfy it more than for Keith to join it in death. Keith picked up the body and admired the heft. It had been a big boy. He looked at the nubby tail.

Keith rode his ATV across his pastures. He rode along the fence line, looking for breaks. Ever since his cattle started coming up with wounds, he'd had to keep a close eye on his fence for loose wires. He didn't know if they were getting broken by his panicking cattle or by whatever was attacking them.

He came to a place where the top wire had snapped and hopped off his ATV. He took his wire tensioner from the tool chest on the back and went to work. A broken fence was always a bad sign. Whatever had broken the fence had bled, on the wire and on the grass.

With the barbed wire mended he got back on his ATV and broke away from the fence line, checking on his herd. They grazed and ignored him. They were accustomed to him and his little four-wheeled vehicle. Most of them had watched him ride around on it since they were born. Keith had done that work on a horse as a young man, but he didn't mind progress.

Eventually he came upon a cow with black dried blood crusted down its neck and front leg. He hopped down and checked it. The cow never stopped chewing the grass as

Keith felt lightly at the wound. There wasn't much to be done. The cow was fine. The holes had already closed up on their own. Still.

Keith rode on. He had a feeling. He headed away from the herd, back to the fence line. He wasn't sure how he knew, but he knew, and felt no surprise when he came upon a cow lying on its side. The other cow's neck had merely been punctured. This one's was torn open. Low on the shoulder were large deep claw wounds. He checked for signs of life but of course there were none. Dead. Keith shook his head.

"Shit."

CHAPTER 2

Sheriff Wheeler, tall and lanky, walked with a group of men across Logan's pasture. Old Mr. Logan, angry, hunched and dried-out, led the way. Behind them came Gerald Rossford, a Kansas State University professor who headed a state-funded project to research the animal attack issue, and his graduate assistant, known to Sheriff Wheeler only as Jason.

"The latest is right over here," Mr. Logan said. He pressed through the waist-high, stiff grass like it was running water. He was a cantankerous old bastard and got on a lot of people's nerves, but Sheriff Wheeler couldn't help but find him funny. "At least as far as I know. Probably half my herd laying dead around here."

They came upon a steer collapsed on its side. Like most of the others, its neck had been torn and it lay in a dried pool of its own blood. Dr. Rossford knelt down beside the carcass and examined the wounds.

"So what are we dealing with here?" Sheriff Wheeler asked.

"Well, that's hard to say. We know that this isn't the work of any predator on record," Dr. Rossford said.

"So you know that it's nothing that you know of. That's helpful."

Dr. Rossford seemed to catch Wheeler's sarcastic tone. He stood up and faced him. "It's not much, but it's something, and it's actually very exciting. There aren't many predators left in North America capable of killing a full-grown cow. And the number of large predators is constantly reducing, never increasing."

"Doctor, you have to understand that my community doesn't share your enthusiasm for this new predator capable of destroying their livelihood, however interesting it may be to the scientific community. So what can you tell them?"

Dr. Rossford nodded in a way that showed that he understood the plight of the common man. "I can tell you that it's part of a pattern. I've read files on cases like this that started two years ago in Oklahoma. A few years before that, it was Texas. So whatever this creature is, it seems to be expanding its territory north."

"Why?"

"Food supply? Over-population? Global warming? Who knows. But these attacks weren't happening on US soil a decade ago."

"Holy shit," Sheriff Wheeler said, rolling his eyes. "Are you actually telling me that we're dealing with illegally-immigrated chupacabra?"

Dr. Rossford and Jason both laughed. Rossford gestured to Jason. "Don't think we haven't joked about that. Who knows? The Mexican government doesn't do a great job of documenting mythical creatures. It sure does match the creature's MO, doesn't it?"

Sheriff Wheeler felt his annoyance growing. "I'll let the ranchers know how funny the situation is. Can I also perhaps pass on at least a description of what this animal might look like?"

"We can make some educated guesses," Dr. Rossford said, crouching down beside the carcass. Wheeler squatted beside him, feeling his knees crackle in protest. Dr. Rossford spanned his hand across the cow's bloody neck wound.

"Despite what you might think, this isn't a large bite wound. If judging by the size of the bite alone–the width of the wounds inflicted by the upper fangs and the distance between the wounds inflicted by the upper fangs and those inflicted by the lower fangs–I'd say this creature was no bigger than a coyote."

"What? Are you serious?" Wheeler asked.

"That wasn't done by no coyote," Logan said. Wheeler felt the old man's spittle hit the back of his neck as he spoke.

"That's only if you go by the size of the bite. The strength of the bite is considerably greater than that which most animals the size of a coyote could produce. So the predator probably has a small muzzle proportionate to its size. That makes sense, because the purpose of the bite isn't to crush the throat and suffocate, as a cougar would, but simply to puncture the carotid artery or the jugular vein. This allows the predator to drink the blood, like the chupacabra we joked about."

"Yeah, we know all that," Wheeler said. "What new can you tell me?"

"These are your experts?" Logan asked, once again spraying Wheeler's neck with his denture-pickled saliva.

"You need to back up, Logan. Jesus." Sheriff Wheeler wiped the back of his neck.

"Sorry for getting too close to my own dead steer." But Logan took a step to the side.

Dr. Rossford said, "Sheriff, I'm working with the same information that has you and your people stumped. I'm trying to paint you a picture of what this animal might look like based on the limited evidence we have. Are you going to let me?"

"Sorry. Go ahead."

Dr. Rossford leaned closer to Wheeler. "The rest of the information is sensitive. Not for the public. We need to speak privately."

Wheeler slowly stood, pressing down on his creaking knees. "Logan, I'm gonna have to ask you to leave."

"This is my land and that's my dead cow."

"I know, I know. And you'll be the first to hear once I've got more to tell. But right now I'm sure you've got plenty to do."

Logan looked like he wanted to say something, but for the first time that Wheeler could remember, he didn't. He turned and walked back towards his house.

"So it has a small mouth," Dr. Rossford said," but a disproportionately strong bite. Considering the way it uses its bite, that's not so strange. What are stranger are its forepaws." The doctor pointed to one set dug into the steer's shoulder. "These upper claw marks aren't that unusual, in that there are four roughly side-by-side. The spacing and depth of the wounds indicates a very large predator, probably near five hundred pounds. The predator uses the claws for grasping, not injuring, so it sinks them in and then holds the prey still as it drinks its blood. And it doesn't always use them. They're found most often in cases where the livestock has been killed, as if they are a sign of over-stimulation in the predator. The strange part about this animal's forepaw is the fifth claw mark. The fifth claw is very far away from the rest, and, if you notice the curve of the wound, it faces the opposite direction."

Dr. Rossford looked at Wheeler expectantly, but Wheeler was lost. "Meaning?"

"Meaning this thing has opposable thumbs, or something like them. Now, big cats have dew claws, and they are sizeable, but they face mostly in the same direction as the other claws. So could this be a new type of large cat? I don't think so, but it's being considered. There are marsupials with opposable thumbs–"

"Now I know no possum did this," Wheeler said.

Dr. Rossford laughed. "Very true. I don't think some enormous mutant opossum is responsible for this. The point I was making is that the strangest thing about this new predator isn't its thumbs."

"Oh, great. So what's the strangest?"

"The venom," Jason said, smiling.

Dr. Rossford nodded. "The venom. It's a neurotoxin. It sedates the prey, which is why the use of claws seems to be optional and a sign of over-eager feeding. Because the animal typically bites the neck, the venom goes straight to the brain and begins working in less than a second. The toxin affects the brain rather than the peripheral nervous system, and it appears to cause permanent damage. It's difficult to tell with cattle because, well, they're cattle. But the strangest thing about the venom–"

"You know, you really seem to be enjoying this. There's always a new 'strangest thing' around the corner. Is this finally it?"

"The strangest thing is that the venom contains a microorganism, similar to a virus."

"That's not so strange. I saw something like that on a show about Komodo dragons."

"Very good, Sheriff. But this isn't the same. Komodo dragon saliva is filled with bacteria which live in their mouths. This appears to be a new sort of microorganism, not quite a virus. Every member of this species seems to be infected with it, at least judging from the bite wounds we've taken samples from. In fact, it appears that the animal may have a symbiotic relationship with the microorganism."

"So it infects its prey?"

"No. That's what's so interesting. The cattle that have survived attacks show no signs of infection, despite the infectious agent being present in the wounds. The agent can't survive in the cows' blood, only in the venom at the wound site. We've got a few theories going."

"Of course you do." On television, people always picked on nerds. Wheeler had never understood why. He felt that he was beginning to, though.

"It might be a vestigial carry-over. The venom containing the infectious agent works, so the agent hasn't been evolved out even though it doesn't do anything. Or– and this is the more interesting possibility–"

"You'll like this," Jason the graduate assistant said.

"Cattle might not be its natural prey. A particular virus is able to infect only a particular type of animal. For instance, you can't catch a cold from your dog. A virus has to mutate to jump species."

"Like the bird flu they keep worrying about," Wheeler said.

"Exactly. Since this predator seems to be migrating, it might be encountering food sources it's not fully adapted for."

"So what's its natural prey?" Wheeler asked, finally getting into the mystery. "What should it be infecting?"

"Who knows? That's why it's so interesting."

"Some people would call that interesting. Most would call it a bit anti-climactic." Sheriff Wheeler held out his hand and Dr. Rossford shook it. "Thank you for talking to me, but I've got a Ranchers' Association meeting to get to."

"Hopefully next time we talk, I'll have a little more to tell you."

"That'd be good. Please do keep me in the know. These ranchers are halfway up my ass."

Wheeler tipped his hat and walked away.

CHAPTER 3

Keith stepped out of the bathroom, rubbing his hair dry with a towel. He looked at himself in the mirror over his wide dresser. He pushed his stomach out and smacked it with both hands, then sucked it in. Not bad. Not bad for nearing fifty. For the crap he ate and the way he drank. But the alcohol had recently been taking his appetite.

He got dressed. Clean, dark blue jeans. Western shirt. He checked himself in the mirror again as he cinched up his bolo tie, then sat on the edge of the bed. For a moment he felt the cool softness of the quilt with his palms. Irene had made it. It had taken her quite a while. She'd also embroidered the country scenes onto the decorative pillows at the head of the bed. She used to sit on the porch and cross-stitch and hum tunelessly. No one had ever been brave enough to tell that woman she was completely tone-deaf.

Keith leaned down and grabbed one of his dress boots. His lower back tightened in protest. It wanted to punish him for riding the ATV over the little ridges along his property all morning. He slipped the boot on.

In the kitchen Keith sat a beer on the counter and cracked it open. He lifted it to his mouth and drank half of it down at once, then stopped to catch his breath. The cold tightened up his throat. Once it opened again he gulped the rest down, crushed the can and tossed it in the trash. Then he ducked into the fridge for another. He set it on the counter and cracked it open.

Keith drove past small houses with toys littering their front yards, then past mostly abandoned brick buildings. He stopped at the town's only traffic light. It had one color–red–and it flashed continuously. He looked over at the gas station that warranted the traffic light and noticed the beat-up van parked beside the trucks. Brandon and Dennis were there. Keith wondered if they'd still be after the meeting. He drove on.

He pulled into the gravel lot outside the community center and parked alongside the other pickups. The gravel crunched under his boots as he got out and walked up to the door, converging with the other men. Some ignored him, others nodded to him. He returned the nods.

"County Ranchers' Association meeting, June 6th, 7 PM" was written on the chalkboard beside the door, beneath a small awning.

Keith paused inside and scanned the large room. The community center had a storage room and a kitchen, but was otherwise one large gathering hall. He looked around the clusters of talking ranchers. At the other end of the building stood a small stage with a podium. Behind the podium was the couch that Santa sat on during the community Christmas celebration. He hadn't been to one since Irene died. She'd enjoyed watching the children sit on Santa's lap to tell him what they wanted that year. Female problems early on left her unable to have children, but she'd been the mothering sort.

From the folding chairs facing the stage, Keith's younger brother Roy waved at him. Roy was shorter and plumper than Keith. He took after their mother, who'd been a kind woman. Keith walked over and took the seat beside him.

"How're things, brother?" Roy asked.

"'Bout the same as ever."

"I hear ya. Can you believe they scheduled this at the same time as the game?"

Keith shrugged. "Not like we'll win."

"I think we might. I was watching ESPN and they—"

"We won't win, Roy."

"You don't know that. I heard that—"

But the click of a microphone and a violent burst of feedback silenced Roy and all the other ranchers. Dale, the Ranchers Association president stepped away with his hands up, as if to pacify the sound system. The screeching stopped and he took a tentative step back toward the podium and said, "This meeting of the Ranchers Association will come to order. First, if the secretary would please read the minutes of the last meeting..."

Keith slouched down into the folding chair. It provided no support for his aching back. He thought mostly about this until Dale said, "And Sheriff William Wheeler has been kind enough to agree to speak to us about the animal attack issue."

Keith sat up in his seat. So did Roy. So did everyone else. Some people began to mutter, until Dale loudly said, "Let's please give him our attention while he speaks. He's agreed to answer a few questions afterwards."

Sheriff Wheeler walked up to the podium. He gripped it with both hands and looked uncomfortable. "First off, I want it to be known that we're all on the same side here. You all know that I've got a few cattle—"

The murmuring started up again, angrier than before, but Sheriff Wheeler raised his voice over it. "—that I've got a few cattle myself. I might not make my living at it like you all do, but I also have a personal stake. Several deputies also have cattle. What I'm saying is that we're all on the same side. We're doing the best we can. The government has sent some animal experts to determine what exactly is attacking the cattle, and—"

"So you still don't know?" someone shouted.

From the side of the stage where he sat in a folding chair Dale shouted back, "Let Sheriff Wheeler speak first and he'll answer questions afterwards."

Sheriff Wheeler held up his hand toward Dale. "It's alright. No, we don't know what it is yet—"

The crowd became loud again, but Wheeler continued, "—but we're confident we'll know soon. These guys seem on the ball. Real sharp. All we can do right now is buckle down, try to watch our cattle and wait for them to do their jobs. Oh, and not do anything stupid." Wheeler pointed out into the audience. "I'm looking at you, Jim."

That got some laughs, and he continued. "We don't know what's out there, so seriously: don't act stupid. Okay. Are there any questions?"

There were a lot of questions.

Even after Sheriff Wheeler left the stage, men surrounded him, asking him the same things over and over. Keith wasn't interested in hearing anymore, especially not from Wheeler. Wheeler had talked a lot and hadn't said much, as Keith had known he would.

Keith and Roy walked past the men clustered around Wheeler as they headed out of the building. Ken Rockwell was saying, "I can't afford to lose anymore cattle."

"Do you think any of us can?" Wheeler said, clearly exasperated.

"That's not what I'm saying. All I'm saying is that I can't. I just can't." That got a lot of nods all around. Keith had to smile. Wheeler looked ready to pop.

Wheeler looked up just in time to see Keith smile and glared at him. Keith held his gaze for awhile but kept walking. He didn't have anything to prove.

Keith crunched through the gravel and opened his truck door. "See ya, Roy."

"Hold on a second. Sheila told me to invite you over for supper tomorrow night. She's been asking about you."

"That's very nice. Tell Sheila hi for me."

"You can tell her yourself tomorrow night."

"You heard Wheeler. We need to keep our eyes on our cattle."

Roy huffed. "So that's gonna be your excuse now? Keith, what you need is to get out of that house every now and then. I'm your brother and your damn next door neighbor and I haven't seen you in a week."

Keith could see that Roy was waiting for a response, but he gave none. He didn't like explaining himself.

"Come over," Roy said. "Sheila misses seeing you."

"Tell Sheila I appreciate the invitation, but I can't. Go catch the end of the game."

"Fine, you stubborn old bastard. I'll be seeing you."

Keith nodded and stepped up into his truck, then suddenly remembered something. Leaning out the window he said, "Hey Roy."

"Yeah?"

"Tell Jessica to come by tomorrow. I've got something for her."

"You could give it to her at supper."

Once again Roy waited for a response, then finally said, "Fine. I'll tell her."

Keith nodded. His truck roared to life and he backed out. He needed to get some beer before heading home.

CHAPTER 4

Dennis saw all the pickups headed for the community center and knew that Keith would drive past sooner or later. He tried not to pay any attention. But every time a truck went by he was reminded of Keith, and every time he got reminded of Keith he felt the compulsion to adjust his dead left arm, until soon he was watching the road and holding his arm and could barely pay attention to anything else, even though the evening had started out good, sitting and smoking and bullshitting with his friends.

So he noticed when Keith drove by, and it blanked his mind. He'd been talking, but he flushed and stopped.

"So what happened next?" Brandon asked.

Dennis pulled himself back. He was sitting on the curb in front of the QuickStop. Even though he was nearly thirty, he was surrounded by a group of mostly older teens listening to him talk about this movie he'd seen the week before. He brushed his long, stringy hair out of his face, then adjusted his arm. He wished he'd just worn his sling, but he felt self-conscious about it. When he didn't want people to think about his arm, he held his hand in his lap when he sat and put it in his pocket when he stood.

"Oh, yeah. So the dude has his hands behind his head like they've got the drop on him and he knows it's all over, right? Wrong. He's got this stockless shotgun in some sort of holster that runs straight up his back, and he pulls it out and starts blasting. He runs right into the middle of them and is popping their heads from like, inches away, and they can't shoot him because they'll shoot each other. He drops like six guys in about that many seconds."

Brandon laughed. "Badass, man!"

Dennis considered Brandon to be his lieutenant. He was big, loyal, in his early twenties and not going anywhere. And he always played up Dennis's stories. They lived together, so Dennis had already described that scene to him like twice, but he acted like it was new every time. He was a good guy.

"Oh yeah," Dennis said. "And the dude's stone cold. He's standing in this pile of corpses, like, covered in blood, and he doesn't even bat an eye."

The kids all nodded and listened with rapt attention. Normally he would have loved that. Hell, it was probably half the reason he stayed in that shithole instead of moving to Wichita. He liked being a big fish in a small pond. He liked the fact that there, being a small-time drug dealer gave him status, while in any sizeable place he'd be a joke. The kids graduated or dropped out of high school and maybe hung around for a few years before moving away, but there was always a new pack to impress and he liked it that way. But seeing Keith had thrown him off, and he was annoyed with them.

Brandon said, "Is that still playing?"

"Should be. I'd watch it again."

Some of the kids started talking about going to see it, telling Dennis to call them if he went, but he'd just caught sight of Jessica Harris walking up. She was still in high school, but so hot. When she got older, she might turn into a hatchet face, but just then she was incredible. She was Keith's niece, and actually looked more like him than her dad, with his sharp features and hard eyes. But her youth softened all that. And her legs were so damn long. Dennis had to wonder if he were a bit sick being so hot for a girl who looked like the man who'd crippled him. Like Stockholm syndrome or something. But even if she weren't jailbait, and even if she weren't Keith's niece, he still wouldn't go for her, because she and Brandon had had a thing and he still moped over her like some big, stupid dog.

She was completely ignoring them, heading for the door, when one of the punk kids said, "Hey, Brandon, here comes your girl."

"That's not his girl," Dennis said. He turned to see who had spoken. Jim Kroger, a runt skater asshole who bought weed off him whenever he could steal enough money from his parents.

"Not anymore," Brandon said.

"Fuck right not anymore."

Jessica walked past them and into the store, and the stupid kids chattered. Dennis sat silent and sullen. Brandon stared at the ground.

When Jessica emerged carrying a gallon of milk and a candy bar, that stupid punk Kroger said, "Hey, Jessica!"

Jessica didn't turn around, didn't even pause, just flipped them off over her shoulder, and Kroger started whooping and howling.

Dennis shoved him with his good arm and said, "What do you think you're doing, jackass?"

Kroger fell off the curb where he sat beside Dennis and hopped to his feet aggressively. Dennis didn't bother to stand, just shook his head as Brandon stood up behind him. Brandon had nearly a hundred pounds on the kid. Kroger grabbed his skateboard and started skating around the lot. Roger, the QuickStop owner, hated when he did that.

Brandon sat back down. "Fucking kids."

The other kids were quiet. Dennis put a cigarette in his mouth, then lit it.

Dennis had mostly forgotten his bad mood, and was animatedly telling a story of a meth lab that blew up a month or so before when the pickups started to go past again, this time headed out of town. A few minutes later, Keith pulled up in his giant, dirty Ford. Dennis desperately wanted to go hide. Even though there had been no reason to think that Keith would stop at the gas station, Dennis wished he'd followed his coward's instincts and left.

The kids barely noticed Keith until Brandon got up and stood near the door, staring at Keith as he walked past. Dennis didn't move from the curb, but watched Keith and smiled. That was the most he could manage, though when Keith met his eyes Dennis's dropped to the ground and his smile vanished and he smoked his cigarette like it required all his attention.

Keith threw the door open, nearly hitting Kroger, who'd sat back down.

"Hey!"

Brandon stood outside the door, glaring in. Dennis wanted to tell him to stop fucking around, to move out of Keith's way, to not bring any more of his attention on them, but he couldn't. Not in front of the kids. Dennis was a drug dealer. He was ten years older than a lot of them. They looked up to him. He didn't have to get in Keith's face himself, but he couldn't tell Brandon to lay off of him.

Keith appeared on the other side of the door, holding a twelve-pack of beer.

Dennis stood and stepped back, hugging his left arm nervously. Keith gave Brandon a moment to get out of the way of the door, but when Brandon crossed his arms, he shoved it open hard, knocking Brandon back and making him stumble. Brandon recovered and got in Keith's face.

Dennis's heart pounded high up in his chest. He needed Brandon to be aggressive, but just then he wished he had a choke chain for the stupid motherfucker.

"You should go home, old man," Brandon said.

"Planning on it." He shouldered past Brandon, making him stumble yet again.

Keith opened his truck door and hopped up into his seat, leaning across and setting down the beer.

Brandon glanced around at the kids, then said, "And tell Jessica hi for me."

The kids laughed. Kroger doubled over, one foot on his skateboard. Dennis wanted to hide. He wanted to run behind the building and down the alley and hide.

Keith froze for a moment, still leaning across the seat. Then he reached for something and got back out. The something was an ax handle.

The kids stopped laughing and stepped away from Brandon, but Brandon didn't move. He wasn't smart, but he was brave. Or he was too dumb to be scared. Dennis didn't know if there was a difference.

"What was that?" Keith asked.

Brandon set his jaw and clenched his fists at his sides.

"Go ahead and say her name again," Keith said.

Brandon didn't move an inch. Didn't look down. Dennis didn't know how someone could have so little sense of self-preservation. Brandon was bigger than Keith, sure, but Keith had proven that he was a brutal maniac, and he was armed.

"Do it Brandon!" Kruger yelled. "Fuck that old man up!"

Keith stepped even closer. Brandon didn't move. Keith leaned way in and whispered something in Brandon's ear. Brandon still didn't move, didn't speak.

Keith took a step back. He snorted, then turned his back to Brandon. He waited, letting the insult set in, but Brandon still didn't move. So Keith walked back to his truck, tossed the ax handle onto the seat, and cool as anything backed out and drove away.

Once he left, the kids circled Brandon, congratulating him, smacking him on the back and generally acting like assholes. Dennis sat back down on the curb.

Soon, Brandon joined him. The teenagers were still worked up, wrestling and pretending to box each other.

"Why do you provoke him?" Dennis asked, not looking at Brandon.

"I just can't let him get away with it. I don't know how you can."

Dennis shook his head, and still didn't look at Brandon. He didn't know whether to say "thanks" or "fuck you." Instead, he asked, "What did he whisper to you, anyway?"

"He said, 'Do it, Brandon. Say her name again. Say Jessica.'"

CHAPTER 5

Keith originally built the porch for Irene, but he had grown to prefer it to the house. He sat in the dark loudly sipping a beer, the twelve pack beside his chair. His dogs lounged around his feet, sleeping. They snored through their wrinkled snouts. The mild night air, the beer and the sound of snoring dogs soothed Keith to sleep.

Keith often dreamed of Irene. He didn't like that he usually dreamed of her sick. They'd had a good life together. He thought she deserved to be remembered better. But he usually dreamed of her sick.

She lay propped up in a hospital bed. He sat beside her holding her hand. She was still pretty. Not yet eaten away and dried up.

"You have to go now. Visiting hours are over," Irene said.

"I can't."

"You have to. I'll see you tomorrow."

"Promise."

"What?"

"Promise that you'll see me tomorrow."

"Keith..."

"You have to promise."

She squeezed his hand and stared at it. She wouldn't look at him.

He said, "If you can't promise, then I can't leave."

"I promise. It's just chemo."

She finally looked him in the eyes. There was guilt on her face. Part of him knew that he was dreaming. Part of him knew that he wouldn't see her tomorrow, because she was already dead. And because part of him knew that part of her knew, too. She knew she was lying, that she'd be gone when he awoke.

But he didn't want to upset her further, so he kissed her on the cheek and said, "Keep your promises," and walked for the door.

Just as he reached the door, Irene said, "Keith?"

He waited, hand on the doorframe. He didn't want to look back at her. He didn't want to have to gather the strength to leave again. He just said, "Yes?"

And she shrieked.

Keith shot to his feet, confused. He was on the porch, not in a hospital room. A beer can hissed out its remaining contents onto the weathered boards. He'd been dreaming, but the scream continued. It wasn't Irene. It wasn't human.

Keith turned his head toward his pasture and noted the direction of the scream before it faded away.

He ran the few steps to his front door, nearly tripping and putting his hands through the glass amidst his cowering, whimpering dogs. They crowded the door and ran inside as soon as he opened it. He reached in and grabbed his shotgun. "Hunting dogs. Yeah."

Keith rode his ATV across his dark pastures. Grass and small shrubby trees whipped past in a white blur, lit for only a second at a time. In his headlights, a cow appeared and he skidded to a stop. Blood poured from a wound on the cow's neck. Keith didn't see the predator until a sudden shriek nearly made him fall backwards from his seat.

The ATV's headlights illuminated the cow, but not the dark shadow perched on its back. It shrieked again. An incredible stench wafted after the sound.

Keith aimed his shotgun at the shadow blocking the stars, but the creature clamped tightly to its meal's back and Keith couldn't get a clean shot. After a moment the shadow hissed and disappeared. Keith heard it hit the ground behind the cow. He fumbled behind him for his flashlight and ran around the cow. He scanned the night with his flashlight and his shotgun, but could see nothing.

He examined the wound. It was deep, but not torn. He went back to his ATV and got a pad of the gauze he'd begun carrying with him since the attacks began. He pressed it against the cow's neck. The blood soaked through, warm and slick. Before long, it began to scab. The bandage stuck and the bleeding stopped.

Keith slouched on the seat of his ATV. He couldn't stop his chin from dropping to his chest. Each time he snapped awake in panic. He spun in his seat, aiming the shotgun out into the darkness. As the intervals between falling asleep grew shorter, Keith finally gave up and rode home.

He sat his shotgun beside the door and trudged past the entry to the living room. He put a boot on the first stair, then walked back. He stepped into the living room and slowly turned.

He didn't live there. He lived on the porch. He ate in the kitchen. He slept in the bedroom. The living room had always been hers; he still didn't live there. He dusted it occasionally. All the little knickknacks and such collected dust. He looked at the pictures on the wall. His favorite was one of them together in Branson. Both smiling. He didn't look at it often.

He went to the kitchen and saw his dogs sprawled around on the cool nylon flooring. He shooed them into the utility room and shut them in. He didn't think any of them would set foot in the living room even while he slept, but it wasn't fair to tempt them. His father hadn't let their dogs inside at all. Keith supposed he was softer than his old man had been. He grabbed a bottle of bourbon and a tumbler from the cupboard and went up to bed.

The next day was hot. Hotter for how dry he felt. He'd knocked back almost half of the liter to help him get to sleep, then slept too late into the day.

The sun sat high in the sky by the time he climbed a ladder up to the roof of his tool shed. Some of the corrugated tin had come loose in a summer storm the week before. He pinched nails between his thin lips. One at a time he pounded them through the tin and into the rafters. He wore a ball cap, but the sun beat down on his neck. The tin was hot enough that it burned him through the thick calluses on his thick hands. The ladder wobbled beneath his feet. And worst of all, the shotgun slung across his back was jostled by every swing of the hammer. He thought that maybe he'd start carrying his .45 instead. Regardless, he wouldn't go unarmed again.

He rode his ATV to a spot along the fence line that he'd noticed the day before. Some scrubby hedge trees had grown quickly in one spot and were taking the barbed wire up with them. When he found the trees he grabbed his small chainsaw and started to work at the thin, thorny branches. Even young Osage orange trees were tough. They grew all along the fields in hedges, delineating the dirt roads and keeping the top soil from blowing away. They were good for this and nothing else. An Osage orange branch never grew straight for longer than a few inches. A fence with posts made from those gnarled limbs was a laughably crooked affair. Because the wood twisted so, it stacked poorly in a stove. You wouldn't want to use it anyway if you didn't want your house to burn down. For some reason, Osage orange wood cracked like firecrackers the entire time it burned, sending out showers of sparks that could make their way all the way up a chimney and onto the roof. He occasionally burned some anyway, and one time had caught a blast of sparks in his eyes while he tended the stove. It made him jerk up so that the backs of both his forearms hit the top edge. Irene said she felt bad for him, but you couldn't tell it from the way she laughed as she treated his burns.

After he finished trimming back the trees, he rode out to where he'd encountered the creature the night before. The sun had toasted the grass yellow-white, so the black stains of blood stood out even more distinctly.

The thing had been loud and it had been big. He wondered if it could be a mountain lion. They weren't common in those parts anymore, but maybe a mother and some older cubs had moved in looking for easy meat. He knew that mountain lions often attacked from above, and would sit on a prey animal's back while it worked at its spine at the base of the skull if it didn't go for the throat.

Keith knelt in the grass and fingered the crusty, stained grass. Then he noticed something on the ground. Stiff and blood-encrusted as well, he had to pry it out of the dried pool. A small, ripped piece of cloth.

Keith sat on his porch in the dark. He drank a beer with one hand. The other rested on a dog's head as it laid its floppy muzzle across his thigh and looked at him with dopy brown eyes. Keith's shotgun stood propped against the other side of his chair.

Keith pondered over the bit of cloth he'd found earlier in the day. There seemed to be only two possibilities: either the piece of cloth had already been there and the predator simply happened to attack the cow as it stood right over it, or this creature attacked both man and beast and had brought the cloth with it, stuck in its fur or some such. The first option seemed very implausible, which left only the second. So Keith felt that he should be scared. He shouldn't go rushing into the night to face off with whatever kept attacking his cattle. But there he sat, shotgun near to hand.

The dogs began to whimper. They crawled to the door with their tails low. Keith hadn't heard anything. He hushed the dogs and listened, trying to hear whatever they were hearing. After a moment, he made out a scream. But it wasn't the same shriek he'd heard the night before. It was further away. And it was human.

Keith raced down the gravel road in his Ford. He gripped the steering wheel tightly in both hands, making small adjustments as the big wheels hit ruts and tried to redirect the truck into the ditch. He slowed after turning onto the paved county road. There was a slight hill, and he stopped before he crested it and pulled over on the tiny shoulder. Grabbing his shotgun, he got out and gently closed the door. As he jogged over the top of the hill, he saw a vehicle parked on the side of the road. He had a feeling that he knew whose it was. As he got closer he saw that it was indeed Brandon's van. He smiled and jogged as quietly as he could manage in his boots.

He crouched down as he approached the van and sidled up, shotgun at the ready. No one sat in the front seats. They must still be at the tanks.

Keith sniffed the air. He didn't smell ammonia. That confused him, but then it made him smile. He ducked under the top fence wire and jogged cautiously toward the tank. He still couldn't see anyone. He stared at the tank, trying to force his eyes to see better in the dark.

The blast of light felt almost physical and Keith cursed under his breath. He forced his eyes to adjust quickly and brought his shotgun up. The tank which had been floating peacefully in the darkness now reflected the security lights brilliantly. Blood splattered the tank and the surrounding grass, much of which had been stomped flat. A Technicolor red handprint stood out against the painful white of the tank.

Keith went home and called for the Sheriff. He knew it would take Wheeler a few minutes to get dressed and drive over, so he opened a beer and drank half of it down. His empty stomach was angry but began to absorb the alcohol immediately. Keith took a long slug of bourbon from the bottle and chased it down with the rest of the beer.

A half an hour later, Sheriff Wheeler and Deputy Thomas pulled up ahead of Keith's truck, which was ahead of Brandon's van. Deputy Thomas flipped the lights on as Wheeler got out and the scene pulsed with the spinning light. Keith stood to meet Wheeler, not liking to sit around the man.

"So what's up this time, Keith?" Sheriff Wheeler asked.

"I told them on the phone. I think someone's been killed."

"And what makes you think that?"

"An awful lot of blood."

Keith led them over to the tank, warning them about the motion-sensitive security lights. They examined the scene. Then Wheeler started asking questions. The first were innocuous, basic, and Keith thought that maybe Wheeler would be decent given the gravity of the situation. But Keith wasn't surprised when the tone soon changed.

"So, you heard a scream all the way from your house? What is that, half a mile?"

"As the crow flies. Almost a mile by road."

"So as far as sound is concerned, half a mile. That's still quite a ways.

"The breeze was blowing my way. I was listening close 'cause my dogs heard it first."

"Okay, so you heard a scream..." He gestured for Keith to continue.

"My first thought was of whatever animal's been getting at the cattle. Then I realized it was coming from my field, not my pastures. And that's when I remembered the fertilizer. I told the co-op it didn't make sense to set it right by the road."

Deputy Thomas walked over holding a small tank up with one gloved hand. Thomas was a big man. "I found this tossed over in the grass. It's empty."

"So he didn't get around to stealing Keith's fertilizer," Wheeler said.

The big deputy gestured over his shoulder to the large tank. "Nope. The security tie is still on the valve. Keith's right. I don't know why they're having people put these tanks right by the road."

"That's the new practice," Wheeler said.

"Just last year they were saying to set them somewhere nobody could find them," Thomas said. "Now they want them out in the open where anybody can get to them."

"These junkies'll find the tanks wherever you put them. At least forcing them to steal right out in the open makes them think twice." Wheeler gestured to Keith, "Anyway, go on."

"After the scream, I thought some druggie had gotten hit with ammonia."

Deputy Thomas nudged Sheriff Wheeler, "Remember Cody Schuller?"

"That was terrible."

To Keith, Deputy Thomas said, "He didn't get the nurse tank secured. Got blasted right in the face. Sucked in a big breath, probably to scream. Kenny Craigston found him dead, his lungs half dissolved and running out of his mouth."

The deputy was a nice man. Big and tough, but willing to hear all sides. Even-tempered, basically. But Keith couldn't share his empathy, and said, "Meth heads get what they deserve."

Deputy Thomas had been clucking in sympathy for Cody Schuller. His expression hardened and he walked away.

"He was only nineteen," Wheeler said.

Keith didn't reply, but waited for the next question. After staring at Keith for awhile, Wheeler eventually asked it.

"So you suspected someone was trying to siphon off your ammonia."

"Yeah, but when I got close, I couldn't smell it. So I kept going. Forgot about those new security lights. Nearly bowled me over."

Sheriff Wheeler gestured to the blood. "And that's what you found?"

Keith nodded. Wheeler closed his notebook and put it in his shirt pocket.

"Keith, we've known each other for a long time."

Keith nodded.

"Ever since grade school."

Keith nodded.

"Which is why I have a hard time believing you. I don't doubt that you'd kill a man you found stealing from you, especially one like Brandon. That's Brandon's van."

Wheeler paused. Keith knew he wanted some sort of reaction. He wasn't going to give him one. He'd wait for a question.

"Everybody knows what you did to Dennis's arm. None of them will say anything because they're scared shitless of you, but we all know it was you."

Still not a question. Keith stared straight into Wheeler's eyes.

"And Roger told me that you got into a little altercation with Brandon outside the QuickStop just yesterday."

Keith gave him nothing and watched Wheeler break first.

Wheeler leaned in, snarling low so that his deputy couldn't hear him. "You're no better than a goddamn animal, Keith. And now that Irene's not around to make you roll over and heel, you're a dangerous animal. And then there's the matter of Irene's death–"

Keith squared up to Wheeler. "You be very careful what you say next."

"Nobody exactly knows–"

"Sheriff, consider your words."

Sheriff Wheeler turned away. When he turned back, he'd regained control, but the hatred sat behind his eyes.

"Be straight with me. Brandon was a low-life junky. You didn't like him. None of us did. He deserved this."

Keith decided to meet him halfway, and nodded.

"Did you do this?"

Keith hated explaining himself, but saw that he was going to have to. He scratched his head and looked at the scene, then turned back to Wheeler. "When I saw Brandon's van, I thought about how he sits all day at the QuickStop, smiling his smart-ass smile. I saw that van, and I thought, 'Now's my chance to smash that rotten grin right down his throat.' So when I got close and didn't smell ammonia, I smiled. You know why?"

Wheeler looked confused. "No. Why?"

"Because I knew he'd be conscious for the beating I was about to give him. I know you don't like me. You've got plenty of reason. But I wouldn't have killed him. Not because he wouldn't deserve it, but because I'd rather beat the Hell out of him and then let him serve out a meth-cooker's sentence in Federal prison, where his punk ass would have gotten raped raw on a daily basis."

Keith could see Wheeler's mind working. He saw the reluctant admission that yes, Keith was cruel enough to think just such a horrible thing.

Wheeler nodded. "Okay. Fine. I believe you. At least, until I have a reason not to."

Keith felt a little thankful for Wheeler dropping the issue of Irene, for not forcing him to hurt him. He knew his silence unnerved people, so in thanks, he tried to get more talkative. "I notice we've been talking about Brandon like he's dead."

They both looked at the blood around the tank, now dried burgundy even in the intense light.

"Nobody bleeds this much and survives," Wheeler said. "We'll search the property. Make sure he didn't crawl off somewhere to die. I think whoever did this probably took him."

Keith shrugged. "No big loss."

"Nope. Okay. We don't need you here for this."

"You sure?"

"Yeah. We won't find anything. If we do, I'll come knocking."

"Sheriff?" Deputy Thomas said. Keith had almost forgotten he was there. They both turned and looked at him.

The big man was peering into the windshield of Brandon's van, his flashlight pressed against the glass. "Sheriff, there's something moving in there."

"Brandon?"

Deputy Thomas drew his gun and aimed it at the windshield. "You in the van, come out slowly!"

Something exploded out of the back door of the van. But before anyone could make it around, before anyone could even react, it was gone.

"What in the Hell was that?" Wheeler asked.

CHAPTER 6

Earlier that night, the few streetlights of the town disappeared behind Brandon and Dennis as Brandon drove them into the dark countryside. Dennis's nerves had him looking for people who weren't there. He and Brandon were the only people on the road.

"I hate this shit," Brandon said.

It was weird, seeing Brandon that nervous. Nothing much spooked him. But raw, pressurized, fertilizer-grade ammonia wasn't an enemy you could stare down. It made the old boys at the co-op nervous, and they weren't working with scavenged equipment, in the dark, and clumsy from fear of the law appearing at any moment.

"I thought you were tough," Dennis said. He smiled and reached over, giving him a friendly punch. The fact that he had to twist in his seat because the arm on Brandon's side didn't work annoyed him. The world was full of little reminders like that. It found ways to let him know that he was no longer whole. "I don't like it either, but this deal pays off big."

Their meth supplier, Rob, cooked the best shit in the whole county. Consequently, he also smoked a lot of the best shit in the county, and got real paranoid about leaving his ten-acre plot. Especially when it came to stealing the fertilizer he needed to make his product. So he offered a deal to a few small-timers. If Dennis provided him with raw materials, Rob didn't sell his product to anyone else in Dennis's territory. Dennis knew that it wasn't a big market to corner, but he liked being *the* guy. It added to his status.

The situation provided another opportunity, too. They had to steal the fertilizer from someone, so Dennis figured they might as well steal it from Keith. It wasn't much, but it was something, especially after the confrontation at the gas station.

That year, Keith was keeping his fertilizer right at the edge of his property along the county road. It made the tank easy to find, but it also made Dennis nervous. Someone driving back into town could easily see them from the road. Especially because Keith had put the tank as far from the gravel roads that flanked his property as he could, giving them nowhere to park. The county road had almost no shoulder, so Brandon had to pull as far down into the ditch as he could without rolling the van. Anyone driving past would immediately know something was up, and almost certainly know that they were the ones up to it, since everyone in the area knew Brandon's vehicle.

"This sucks," Brandon said.

"So let's do it quick."

They crept from the van, down the ditch and up the steep opposite side. Brandon slipped between the top and middle strands of barbed wire, then turned around and held the wires apart so that Dennis could follow him through. Dennis wore his sling, but still gripped his bad arm with his good one, not trusting it to stay put as he ducked under the wire. He had neither control nor feeling in the arm, and if it slipped loose and snagged on the barbs he wouldn't even feel it.

God he hated Keith so much.

The big white fertilizer tank glowed in the moonlight, and they ran for it in a crouch. That part of the field was grassy, but it had been plowed before, and uneven ruts still striated the earth. Though the tank sat only thirty or so yards from the fence, Dennis nearly fell on his face several times.

Dennis was mentally preparing himself for the dangerous operation they were about to perform when the world suddenly went white and disappeared. Pain stabbed into his eyes and he clamped them shut and clapped his good hand over them. Beneath his hand, his vision faded from white to shifting stains of every color.

"Goddamn," Brandon said.

Dennis managed to take his hands away from his eyes and saw incredibly bright lights mounted on the tank carriage. "Shit, we gotta do this quick." Now surefooted with the ground fully illuminated, Dennis jogged over to the fertilizer. "Bring the tank over."

"Uhhh..."

Dennis turned around and looked at Brandon's empty hands. "You forgot the tank!"

"I'm sorry. I'm nervous."

"Go get the tank, fast."

"With the lights? Maybe we should just–"

"Shut up and do what you're told, jackass. Go get the tank. And run."

Brandon ran for the van. He was tall and athletic, and could really move. Dennis leaned over the valve. The key would be to be sure their connections were secure before turning that valve. As long as there were no leaks, they'd be fine.

Only a few seconds later, Dennis heard Brandon running up from behind. He felt bad for yelling at him, but sometimes he had to. He didn't think Brandon held it against him. Still. "Way to hustle. Let's get this done."

But the running feet didn't slow, and Dennis turned just in time to see a white blur plow into him, knocking him to the ground. He screamed and tried to drag the thing off him with his one hand, but he couldn't get a grip on it. It moved so much, so fast, and even though its limbs were long and thin, it was strong. In just a moment, it had buried its–face?–muzzle?–into Dennis's neck and bit down. Dennis's vision went black for a moment as he felt the mouth suck powerfully, drawing away blood intended for his brain. It was so alien, to feel the blood being pulled out of his body that way, that he finally stopped screaming.

"Hey! Get off of him!" Brandon shouted.

Over the creature's shoulder, Dennis watched Brandon bring the nurse tank back like a really thick aluminum baseball bat, then slam it against the thing's head. The noise was a combination of a sickening crunch and a gong.

Brandon leaned over Dennis, mouth agape. He reached down towards Dennis's neck. "Oh my God. It bit you good. We gotta get–"

Dennis watched the creature arc through the air and land on Brandon's back, and the sight, in the incredible brightness of the security lights, broke him. Ribs and limbs glowed incandescent from the lights. Black crust covering its face blended into the void of night behind it. But the teeth, the ring of fangs floating in that void until they sank into Brandon's shoulder... God.

As Dennis scrambled to his feet, he saw Brandon grab two handfuls of the thing's hair and yank it over his shoulder. It landed on its back on the ground and shrieked and writhed, but Brandon was on it, smashing it with his fists. Dennis finally got his feet beneath him and ran.

He made it to the van. Brandon had left the back doors open when he got the nurse tank, and Dennis crawled in and pulled them shut behind him. He scrambled to the front and hit the button to lock all the doors. Then he crawled into the windowless back. His head pulsed, swelling out until he thought it would burst, then contracting until the world was only a pinpoint. Something wrenched at the sliding-door handle, then started pounding at the door.

"Dennis! Let me in!"

The keys hung from the ignition.

The pounding and the shouting continued for some time. Dennis couldn't say when it stopped, but at some point it did.

The world continued to get stranger. It faded in and out. It expanded and contracted. He crawled up to the front of the van and looked at himself in the rearview mirror. His skin had lost every bit of color. His hair and skin were slicked with sweat. But it was his eyes that scared him. The pupils dilated until his irises disappeared, then kept dilating, until they were nearly solid black. That seemed impossible. Then, the world contracted, and he felt himself slipping away. It finally pulsed back, but he could tell that he was losing himself. His mind trudged along slowly. He wasn't sure why, but he thought of the plastic baggie of meth he kept in the toolbox. He crawled back and fumbled with the latch. The world closed in again. He felt himself slipping into the darkness and he didn't know if he'd come out. If it was like anything, it was like ODing on heroin.

Meth would help.

With his vision going, he pulled out the baggie and ripped it open onto the corrugated metal floor of the van. He took a hammer from the toolbox and crushed a rock of meth into something like a powder. As the world shrank to a pinpoint, Dennis knelt all the way down to the floor of the van as if in prayer or supplication and snorted the coarsely crushed speed.

His head snapped back and he shot upright. Every muscle in his body contracted as if he were being electrocuted. He felt each muscle shift beneath his skin. But his sight returned. He returned. And he knew what he had to do.

His head still pulsed, but he forced it to expand. Every time it tried to contract, he took another bump. He laughed at the idea of a 'bump.' He was inhaling piles the size and consistency of a packet of raw sugar, taking hit after hit until the blood pouring from his nose made it hard to find a place on the van floor dry enough that the crystals didn't stick.

Finally he sat back against the van wall. The world calmed. It no longer rushed at him. It no longer flew away. It no longer tried to swallow him.

He listened to his heartbeat. It had been racing so that he thought it would explode, but then it slowed. The roar of blood in his ears grew less and less. His breath no longer came in choking gasps, but sips.

His muscles stopped vibrating. His lungs stopped pumping. His heart stopped beating. Dennis was completely still. A corpse.

Until a beam of light slid over him and he flipped into a crouch in one fluid movement and hissed.

"Sheriff, there's something moving in there."

"Brandon?"

"You in the van, come out slowly!"

Dennis ran at the rear doors, and he didn't stop. Somehow he knew that he didn't have to. He exploded through them and landed on the ground in a crouch. One of the doors landed beside him. He sucked in the night air, found what he was looking for, and ran.

CHAPTER 7

Keith sat on his porch, drinking a beer and flicking a large pocket knife open and shut with his free hand.

It was late afternoon. Keith had done what had to be done for the day and didn't feel like doing more. When he was younger he couldn't put a chore off. It had annoyed Irene to no end. Now he'd gotten lazy and she wasn't even there to enjoy it. Anyway, he'd been up late the previous night. He'd just started to doze off as he heard a car approaching, one with a big engine going way too fast. He whipped his folding knife into a porch post, stood and smiled.

An old Pontiac Firebird swung into the driveway and slid to a stop in front of the porch. Jessica climbed out.

"Who taught you to drive these dirt roads like that," Keith asked.

"You did, when Dad wasn't looking."

Keith laughed, and Jessica gave him a quick hug before they both settled into chairs.

"It's been awhile," Keith said. "You can't come visit your uncle when you live right next door?"

"Far as I know, that dirt road's a two-way. I hear you turned down our dinner invitation the other night."

Keith leaned back and took a long drink of beer. "I like to stay close to home anymore. But you should come by."

"Why?" she asked, gesturing to his beer. "So I can sit around watching you pickle yourself?"

Keith raised an eyebrow. He hadn't expected that. Apparently his brother had been talking.

She winked. "Toss me one."

Keith did. She cracked it away from herself, then took a sip.

"But seriously," she said. "I only came around 'cause I heard you've got something for me."

"Ouch."

"Nothing in this world is free, my dear uncle."

"When did you get so cold and calculating?" he asked.

Her expression didn't change. She took another loud sip.

"Makes me proud," Keith said. "Just a second."

Keith went into the house and grabbed her present. When he returned to the door, Jessica stood at the edge of the porch, looking out over the pastures. Keith watched her for a moment. She'd gotten too grown up. He hated to think of her out in the world, away from her parents' protection, from his. But he felt so relieved that she still seemed to like him the way she always had. Like any teen, she'd grown away from her mother and father, but she treated him just the same. It really was a dangerous world when you felt that your life depended on the affection of a fickle teenage girl.

He stepped out onto the porch, keeping both his hands behind his back. She turned around and saw this and raised an eyebrow.

"What're you up to?"

He smiled. "Close your eyes."

"No. You're smiling too much."

Keith shrugged. "Then no present."

"Come on."

"Nothing in this world is free, my dear niece."

"When did you get so cold and calculating? Fine." She huffed and closed her eyes.

"Okay, look."

He held the rattlesnake skull right in front of her face. She screamed and stepped back, but had been standing right at the top of the steps. Her arms pinwheeled for a moment before she fell down the few stairs and landed on her butt in the dirt.

Keith laughed and laughed. Through the tears in his eyes, he could only just make out her face quickly changing from shock to bright red anger. She leapt to her feet and back up the steps and began to beat Keith around his head. Stooped in laughter he was completely unable to defend himself. He could only turn his back and continue laughing.

"You asshole! I could've broke my neck!"

"Sorry," he said. "Sorry!"

Eventually she stopped hitting him.

"What the Hell do I want with a snake skull anyway?" she asked.

Keith finally managed to catch his breath. "The skull's not yours. It was just sitting beside your present and when I saw it I couldn't pass up the opportunity."

Jessica hit him again.

"Okay, okay, stop!"

She put her hands on her hips and scowled at him.

Keith said, "It's amazing to me that you aren't a blood relation of Irene. You remind me so much of her sometimes. She punched like a little girl, too."

She drew back her fist and he said, "Kidding. Don't you want your present?"

"What is it? A live spider? Maybe a booger? Which of us is the adult again?"

Keith held out his hand. He had a bit of fine chain wrapped around one finger. He opened the hand and let the necklace drop. At the end was the snake's rattle.

He said, "The skull and this were sort of a matching set. I figured we could each keep part."

Jessica took the necklace and looked at it closely. She shook her head. Keith worried for a moment that she didn't like it.

"This is so damn cool." She tossed her long hair aside and put it on. "You know, you're the only person who ever gets me anything cool. Thank you."

She hugged him.

"You're welcome."

"So what's its story?"

"Nothing exciting. Came out the other day and saw the dogs bouncing around, barking at this rattler. So I got my shotgun and blasted it in half." He smiled. "I ate the rest in a stew."

"Liar."

"I was gonna save you some but it was really good."

Keith sat down again and she leaned against the porch rail. Keith said, "Supposedly, when you wear that you're protected from venomous creatures."

"Oh yeah? I could use that." Her smile faded a bit, then returned. "What about the skull?"

"I'm not sure. Actually, I think it's bad luck to keep the skull."

"Wonder why."

"Probably because a dead snake will still bite for a time."

"Really?"

"They bite reflexively, even after they're dead."

"Huh."

"That rattle still works, if you shake it fast enough."

Jessica shook the rattle hard, then set her jaw and shook it harder. It made a very slight rattling sound.

"You'll have to work on that," Keith said.

"I really like it."

"I'll remember that you enjoy receiving dead animal parts as gifts."

Jessica laughed. "We're a couple of sick bastards."

Keith chuckled, too. They both sipped their beers.

"Anyway, how's summer school?"

"Hasn't started. Got another week."

"Been applying to colleges?"

"Come on. I talk about this bullshit enough with my parents. We can do better."

Keith nodded. "Okay."

She raised one eyebrow. "How about we discuss that little altercation you had with Brandon at the QuickStop?"

"I wouldn't call it an altercation. We had a friendly chat."

"I heard you almost planted a friendly ax handle upside his skull."

"That's an exaggeration."

"Why don't I believe you?" She smiled, but it faded quickly. "Keith, you have to chill out. I get scared for you."

He scoffed. "You think I can't manage them?"

"No, I think you can't manage yourself. I think you're gonna put someone in a grave and get hauled off to prison."

Keith stared out across his pastures and sipped his beer.

This seemed to aggravate Jessica and her tone got harsher. "Do you want to leave me here alone? You're the only person I can talk to in this shithole."

Keith looked at her. "I'm sorry." He stared at his beer for a moment. "But I'm not the only one. You can talk to your mom and dad."

He winced at the bark of laughter she let out. It was too sharp for her years.

"Brandon mentioned me," she said.

"Yeah."

"Just tell me you didn't have anything to do with him going missing, because that's what everybody is saying."

He looked into her eyes. "I swear I didn't."

She studied him, but finally nodded. "Okay. But what about Dennis?"

"What about him?"

"He's gone, too. They say he went out with Brandon, but neither of them came back."

"Good."

"That's a terrible thing to say."

"Sometimes the truth is terrible. But tell me, you keep saying 'they say.' Who are you hearing all this from? You'd better not be hanging around those junky losers again."

"No, God! Don't you get it? This is what everyone is saying. Everyone is talking about this, Keith."

Jessica crushed her beer can and stood. "Please promise me that you'll keep away from them."

"I promise."

"You don't have anything to prove. Hell, everybody knows what you did to Dennis."

"People don't know shit and talk too much."

"Sure. Whatever." She started for her car. "Mom wanted me to ask you to come to supper, so I have to get back and eat your share."

He followed her to her Firebird. Keith had convinced Roy to let him buy her that car. Jessica had the t-top off, so he didn't have to lean down to talk to her.

"Hey, you make me a promise too," he said.

"What?"

"Promise me you'll learn how to throw a punch. You're defenseless as a newborn."

Jessica shook her fist at him as she started her car, then spun it in his gravel turnaround.

When she was even with him again he shouted, "Seriously! Like butterfly kisses!"

She flipped him off as she tore down his driveway. He watched her dust cloud move along the gravel road. It drifted up and out and eventually disappeared.

The next morning Keith pulled his tractor from the garage and gave the engine a going-over. When he'd last used it he'd noticed it ran a bit rough. Before doing anything expensive he decided to change the spark plugs to see if that'd solve the problem. Standing on the front tire, Keith leaned down into the open hood, ratchet in hand, twisting out the spark plugs and dropping in new ones one at a time to be sure he didn't get any wires crossed.

After fifteen minutes of this his spine was at the point of revolt. He stood up and arched his back, then wiped away the sweat running into his eyes. Out of habit, he scanned the yard.

He noticed one of his dogs standing on the porch, pissing against the house.

Keith squinted to be sure. It took him a moment to believe what he saw. "What in the Hell?"

He jumped down from the tire and ran for the front porch. He wanted to catch the dog in the act so it knew why it was getting beaten.

But the dog saw Keith coming. It started to slink off the porch, but then turned around and ran back up. It ran back and forth on the porch. Keith could see that it wanted to escape, but it seemed unwilling to step foot in the yard. This started the other dogs milling about the porch, whining and cowering.

Keith grabbed the offending hound by its wide orange collar, shook it and smacked it on a rear thigh, bringing a yelp. "What are you doing? You go in the yard."

He tossed the dog forward, then pushed it off the porch with his boot in its hind-end. But the dog had barely hit the dirt before it turned straight back around and ran past Keith. Keith couldn't believe it. He stood dumbstruck for a moment, then reached for its collar.

The dog growled.

Keith snatched his hand back and set his jaw. His dogs didn't growl at him. Ever. In his mind the dog was already dead. He drew a boot back, but then stopped. He only knew of one thing that scared his dogs more than he did.

Keith stepped into his house and grabbed his shotgun and a leash.

When he came back out, he moved as nonthreateningly as he could.

"Okay, Duke. It's okay."

The dog knew the magnitude of its mistake. It desperately wanted forgiveness. Keith slowly reach out his hand, and Duke slowly wriggled along the porch on his stomach.

Keith hooked the leash to the dog's collar, then stood and dragged him off the porch.

The dog tore up the grass as it pulled to get back to the house. Keith walked it all around his big yard. He maintained two full acres as lawn. It was a lot to mow, but he liked the space. As he walked around the yard, he noticed the dog consistently pulling away from a certain direction. So Keith closed his circuit in tighter and tighter until the dog was frantic and there was no question in Keith's mind where the object of the dog's fear was holed up.

Standing before his storm shelter, Keith dropped the leash and let the dog run back onto the porch.

The shelter was a pre-fabricated little concrete bunker set almost completely underground. The heavy steel door sat at an angle to the ground, neither upright nor horizontal. The doorway was about three foot by three foot. Just big enough that an average sized man didn't need to duck to avoid hitting his head as he walked down the metal steps.

A dilapidated wooden shed had once stood where the storm shelter now was. Beneath the building had been a stone cellar that neither he nor Irene ever set foot in because it was full of spiders and snakes and enough junk that anything else could have been hiding down there, too.

Keith remembered the day that they had decided to get the shelter. The building over the unused cellar had been knocked flat. Several other outbuildings had been, too. For some reason, the tornado had lifted just long enough to pass over their house where they crouched in a hallway beneath a mattress. But it destroyed the yard. Several trees were toppled. Branches and whitewashed wood planks covered the ground.

"Look at this mess," Keith had said.

"Tornado barely missed us." Irene shook her head. "This is it. This is the last straw."

Keith looked at the toppled trees. "At least we'll have plenty of firewood come winter."

"Did you hear me? We can't keep sitting in that hallway hoping the house doesn't get hit. This is Kansas. We need a storm shelter."

"Well, the cellar's gone."

"Doesn't matter. The place was disgusting. We'll get a real storm shelter. One of those concrete jobs. We'll drop one right in the hole."

"We can't afford that."

"Things'll be a lot cheaper all around if we're dead."

"Irene, you're exaggerating again." Keith rolled his eyes, but stopped as soon as he realized he'd done it. Too late.

"What does that fake street sign in the Carlson's yard say?"

"Listen, I understand that you're—"

"What does it say?"

"Tornado Alley."

"I'm calling about a shelter today."

"The phone lines are down. We won't have service for a week."

"Then I'll call in a week!"

"What will people say?"

Irene scoffed. "I knew that's what this was about. You think the guys'll make fun of you."

"Nobody else needs a storm shelter."

"None of them are as smart as us. Half of them probably watched the storm from their porches. Let them sit there like the slack-jawed hicks they are and watch a tornado suck them up. We're getting a shelter. End of discussion."

Keith had indeed caught some flak for it. He didn't like to give anyone an excuse to make fun. He couldn't retort back, because he'd always retorted with his fists. Irene didn't allow that.

Staring at the shelter, he smiled and shook his head.

"Stubborn woman."

But that brought back another memory, and his smile faded. Irene, shrunken and frail in her hospital bed. Him talking to her doctor out in the hallway. The chemotherapy wasn't working, but the doctor wouldn't let a crack of doubt through.

"Be straight with me," Keith had asked. "How much more can she take?"

"Irene is strong. She's a stubborn woman, isn't she?"

The doctor had promised Keith that that would carry her through the next few months of Hell, but it hadn't. Apparently she hadn't been stubborn enough.

So there remained no lingering trace of a smile on Keith's lips as he gripped the steel handle of the steel door. He leveled his shotgun at the door, twisted the handle so that it unlatched, and yanked it open.

The smell hit him with almost palpable force. The door had been constructed so that a tornado couldn't pull it open, and it had kept the stink sealed in. Keith turned his head a bit to the side and brought a hand up to cover his nose and mouth. Holding his shotgun level with the other hand he squinted into the darkness. He couldn't see what was down there. It avoided the bit of daylight let in by the open door.

Keith leaned closer and saw something pale move in the darkness. He grabbed his shotgun with both hands, held it to his shoulder and trained it on the movement. A hiss sounded and then the pale something ran for the stairs.

"Holy shit."

Keith pulled the trigger and fell backwards. The thing had moved so fast. Keith scrabbled back on his butt, kicking at the ground with his boot heels, but nothing came up through the door.

Keith got to his hands and knees and grabbed the shotgun he'd tossed aside in panic. He stood, not quite daring to look down into the darkness again. Instead he stayed back, aiming above the door, where the creature would have to appear if it wanted to attack him.

He'd gotten a better look at the thing than he had when it had sat on his cow's back, but not much better. Long limbed and white. And he'd seen fangs. A huge mouthful of crooked fangs.

Keith waited and calmed himself. His hands stopped shaking. His breathing slowed. The squint came back into his eyes. He didn't flinch when a clawed hand that would have been pale had it not been covered in dried black gore gripped the edge of the doorway. He just trained his gun above the hand and waited for the thing to show more of itself.

But something strange happened. Smoke rose from the hand and Keith heard a distinct sizzling sound. With a piercing shriek, the hand was withdrawn.

Keith waited for another few breaths but knew that the creature would not come out. Looking over his shoulder every few steps, he jogged to his truck and grabbed a flashlight from the tool chest.

Shining the flashlight down the hole, a small part of Keith wanted to run and hide. That small part did. What remained was remorseless. The creature blinked at the light and hissed at him pitifully. He shot it a second time. Then a third. The thing lay twitching on the concrete floor. Keith's Remington semi-automatic shotgun carried the hunting-legal three rounds in the tube. He also kept one in the chamber. He shot it again.

Keith and Roy sat on Keith's porch, sawing at steaks on plates in their laps. For a time, the only sounds were the scraping of serrated metal on ceramic, the chewing of meat and the slurping of beer. The grill at the far end of the porch still smoked a bit.

Keith watched Roy slide his last hunk of steak around in the blood and juice and put it in his mouth. He sat the plate on the railing and leaned back. He chewed slowly, apparently savoring the last bite, and finally swallowed.

"Now that was a steak," Roy said.

Keith nodded. He'd stretched his legs out in front of him and laced his hands over his stomach.

"Most people go their whole lives without tasting a decent steak," Roy said. "You ever think about that?"

Keith shrugged.

"All they get is that stringy, grain-fed crap from the grocery store. Been sitting there for who knows how long before they buy it. Can you imagine?"

"Gotta feel bad for them," Keith said.

"That's the truth. Me, I've got more good beef than I know what to do with. Both my deep freezes are full. I'm giving meat away to anyone who ain't scared to eat it at this point."

"Something still getting at your cattle?"

"Had a steer die the day before yesterday."

Keith nodded and looked out at the setting summer sun. From his porch the horizon was huge. Irene had loved to watch the sunset out there. For a time the brothers sat quietly with their own thoughts, sipping their beers.

"You know, the way you asked that question..." Roy shook his head, then sipped his beer.

"What?" Keith asked.

"The way you asked that question, it sounded like maybe your cattle aren't dying. And it's been awhile since you've mentioned it."

"Everybody's cattle are dying," Keith said.

Roy sat with one eyebrow raised expectantly, waiting for Keith to finish. Keith didn't like that Roy could read him like that.

"Except mine," Keith said.

Roy sat bolt upright in his chair. "I knew it! I can tell every time. So what? What are you holding back? You letting my cattle die to get a better price on yours?"

Roy's mouth was smiling but his eyes weren't. And Keith could tell that his mouth couldn't hold the smile much longer.

"Calm down," Keith said. "That's why I wanted you to come over here tonight. I know what's killing our cattle."

"Are you serious? What?"

Keith looked out at the sky. The sun had fully slipped below the horizon. Only a red glow remained. Keith nodded and stood.

"Come on. This I can't explain. This you have to see."

He led Roy across the yard to his storm shelter, then pulled his keys from his pocket. He'd wound a thick chain through the metal door handle and another metal handle set into the door frame. Unlocking the heavy padlock, Keith pulled the chain out and tossed it aside.

"I don't think I really need this anymore, but why take chances?"

Keith cupped a hand over his nose and mouth in anticipation, and opened the door. Roy clamped both hands to his face, but still gagged at the stench.

"Good Lord."

"Prepare yourself," Keith said. He stepped down onto the first step and reached inside the shelter. A carabiner clip connected another chain to an eyebolt bored into the inside of the concrete wall. Keith unclipped the chain and stepped back out.

"Come out," he said.

A deep-throated growl rumbled out of the shelter.

"Keith, what the Hell?"

"I think he's scared of you. He's gotten pretty obedient," Keith said. Then down into the shelter, "I said out!"

Keith braced himself and pulled the chain hard, walking backwards at first, then reeling it in once he had momentum. A pale humanoid creature stumbled out of the shelter and sprawled on the ground. Roy gasped as it tensed and stared back and forth between the brothers in terror.

Keith lifted the thing from the ground by its thick leather collar. It hissed in his face. Keith set his jaw, pulled the creature in by its collar with one hand and punched it in its distended maw with the other. Then he tossed it to the ground.

On all fours, the thing tried to scurry back into the shelter, but Keith grabbed the chain and jerked it hard. The thing toppled onto its back.

"Stay!" Keith shouted.

The creature seemed to have had enough. It rolled over, got to its haunches, and stayed. But Keith was glad that it had decided to act up. It gave him a chance to show Roy the dominance he had over it.

"What in God's name is that?" Roy asked. He maintained his distance, but leaned forward and ducked down, trying to see its face.

"This is what's been attacking our cattle."

"But what is it?"

"I think it's a vampire."

Roy stood up then and shifted his gaze to Keith. Keith maintained the same expression, knowing that Roy was looking for a smile, a wink, anything that said that Keith was fooling with him.

"Are you serious?" Roy asked.

"Something obviously happened to Brandon when he tried to steal my fertilizer. He died, but he didn't stay dead."

Roy's eyes opened wide. He stepped in closer and dropped down to his haunches to inspect the vampire. Keith pulled Brandon's collar, forcing him to look up.

Roy's mouth worked, but nothing came out. He stood and talked almost as if he were trying to convince not only himself, but Keith. "Oh my God. That's Brandon. Holy shit."

"Yeah, I didn't recognize him at first either, but–"

"What happened to him?"

"I guess the vampires got him. Then he rose from the dead."

Roy scoffed, but his face stayed slack. "Those are just stories. Those aren't real."

"And yet..." Keith said, pulling Brandon's chain.

"But look at him. He doesn't look like Dracula."

"No cape. No tux," Keith said.

But Roy pointed to the end of Brandon's arms. "No hands."

It was true. The pale, muscular forearms ended at the wrist in stumps.

"That was me," Keith said. "He'd gone to ground in my shelter. Makes a good enough tomb for a vampire I guess. I didn't even know what it was when I put a few loads of buckshot in its chest, but I was surprised as shit when it didn't die. I wanted to figure out what it was, so I chained the door and waited for it to weaken. It took a few days. I just kept coming back to check on it. At first it like to have shook the door off its hinges when I shouted at it. But its responses got more and more feeble. Finally, I went down there with my .45 and my hatchet. That's when I first saw that it was Brandon. Chopped off his hands and bashed in his fangs."

Roy stared at him with unmistakable horror. "Keith, that's Brandon. That's a human being."

"Not anymore."

"How do you know he's a vampire?"

"Stinks like a corpse. Dead but moving. Burns in the sun. Drinks blood. Has fangs. Well, had fangs. Need me to go on?"

"Still, that's Brandon."

Keith shook his head. "He's an animal now. There's nothing human left in him. I give him a bowlful of cow's blood every couple of days and he's obedient as a dog. And I noticed something: my cattle stopped getting attacked."

"Because you caught what was attacking them."

"Think before you talk. The problem had been going on for a long time before they got Brandon."

Roy looked abashed. "Okay, you're right. So what then?"

"They're territorial. If I keep my cattle in my near pasture, they're fine. I move them out, they come back with wounds again. I've been testing this theory. It works every time. So I want to help you out, too."

"How?"

"You keep your cattle in your west pasture, I'll keep mine in my east, and we'll build a shed for Brandon between them."

It made perfect sense. Keith waited for the agreement. Instead, Roy looked at Brandon with some mixture of distaste and compassion on his face.

"You don't think we should tell the police?"

"It's a bit late for that," Keith said. "Seeing as how I've mutilated him and kept him chained up."

"But they're trying to figure out what's been killing the cattle. They need to know about this."

"Roy, you know that my inclination has always been to take care of my own business. If I were otherwise inclined, if I had told someone, you wouldn't have a farm right now. The government would have taken all our land, all our contaminated cattle, all our crops. Hell, they'd probably take us, too. Quarantine us for being exposed to these creatures."

"But these things are killing people."

"They've been around a long while and only Brandon and Dennis have disappeared so far. I've gone after them before and they've run off. I think they're afraid of people."

"So why him?" Roy said, gesturing at Brandon.

"Haven't figured that out yet. I can see why they'd take Dennis, a crippled, scrawny meth head. I don't know about Brandon, but good riddance."

"I don't know..."

"How much profit are you making off your cattle? Any at all? Even the ones they don't kill aren't putting on any meat because they're anemic. How long can you last like this? You want to go work in a factory?"

Roy looked at the ground and shrugged. Keith looked at his soft younger brother and got more worked up.

"I'm trying to do you a favor. I could put Brandon between my pastures and protect both of them, but I'm offering to share. I'm done talking about this. You know I don't like explaining myself. Yes or no?"

Roy started to speak, but didn't. He stood silent, his mouth working, looking from Brandon to the ground to Brandon. Keith tried to keep his temper in check with his brother. He knew Roy meant well. He knew that Roy was one of the only people on the face of the Earth who gave a damn about him. But Roy was so damn weak.

"This is farm life. Living on a farm has always been about life and death. This can't be the worst thing you've ever had to do!" Finally, Keith did what he hated doing. He made Roy's decision for him, leaving him guiltless. "We're putting Brandon between our pastures."

Roy nodded, but wouldn't look up at him. "Can we stop calling it Brandon?"

Forcing himself to calm down, Keith said, "Sure, but you have to come up with a name. I've never been good at that."

"How about 'the vampire?'"

"Well, I guess I could have come up with that."

"Those pastures aren't going to be enough for all our cattle for long," Roy said, finally looking at him.

"That's why I've trained my dogs not to fear this thing. We're going to track down another one."

They built the wooden structure right against the fence that separated their properties. It had a dirt floor, but Keith had sunk the four-by-four corner posts deep into the earth and cemented them down. Without hands and without the room to stand or even move that much, Brandon would never be able to work his way out. The structure sat so low that it looked less like a shed than a coffin. The effect was enhanced by the fact that it had a lid rather than a door. Keith was nailing corrugated tin to the heavy wooden lid to keep it from rotting.

"You think it's sturdy enough?" Roy asked. He took a drink from a gallon jug of water.

Keith nodded, several nails pinched between his lips.

"What about the sun? We don't want him cooking out here."

Keith took the last nail from his mouth and pounded it into the tin. "That'd be a real shame."

"You know what I mean. You think this'll keep out the sunlight?"

Keith lifted the lid on its heavy hinges. "Only one way to find out." He looked at Roy.

Roy shook his head and took a step back. "No way. I don't think so."

"Then hold this for me."

"Dang this is heavy," Roy said as he took the weight of the lid from Keith.

Keith climbed in and lay down. "Well?" he said.

"What?" The word came out strained as Roy struggled to keep the lid up.

"Close it."

The lid clunked down suddenly. Inside the shed, Keith shook his head at his soft little brother.

The thing really was a coffin. Not totally dark, though. One gap let in a generous wedge of light. Maybe enough to cook Brandon. Maybe not. But Keith noted its position. Then he lay back and enjoyed the silence.

"How does it look?" Roy asked, muffled by the thick wooden walls.

"Shut up."

"What?"

"Shut up!"

The coffin was hot. Keith crossed his arms over his chest and closed his eyes. It made him chuckle at first. He thought of Dracula, not in a castle in Europe, but in a wooden shed in the middle of the Kansas prairie. Then he thought of Irene.

She'd been lying like that in her hospital bed one day when he walked in. She was so thin and frail that for a second he thought she was really dead. Then she opened one eye, shut it again, and smiled.

"What the Hell are you doing?" Keith walked across the room and sat in his usual chair beside Irene's bed.

"Practicing."

"That's not funny."

"Sorry." She looked a bit angry. "Guess my sense of humor's gotten sick, too."

They sat in silence for awhile, until she finally asked, "How's the farm?"

"You know how it is," Keith said, still hurt.

"Yeah."

Keith took her hand and forced the anger away. She was acting out because she was scared. He couldn't hold that against her. "How are you feeling?"

"You know how it is."

"No, I don't."

"It hurts."

"Bad?"

"Pretty bad. And," she looked down and smoothed her thin blanket, "I don't think it's going to get better."

"Please don't say that."

"I'm sorry. I'm not happy about it either."

"You can't leave me."

"I thought this was about me." She smiled weakly.

"No. This is about me. You can't leave me."

"I know. I'm sorry. What do you want me to do?"

"You've always taken pride in being so damned stubborn; so be stubborn. Fight."

She nodded. "It just hurts."

"Roy, I thought I saw your brother over here." It was Wheeler's voice.

Sweat poured down Keith's face. The little box had grown extremely hot. He smacked the lid with his palm, then helped press it up as Roy lifted it.

Keith climbed out. He glared at Sheriff Wheeler as he dusted himself off. He was drenched in sweat. It had soaked the back of his shirt, and the dirt clung to it and refused to be slapped away. Wheeler watched Keith with a smirk on his lips. Keith glared right back.

"Now what were you doing in there, Keith?" Sheriff Wheeler asked.

"Checking for holes," Roy said.

"And what exactly are you two building here?"

Roy slapped the lid. "It's a sort of a tool shed."

"And why are you putting it way out here?"

Roy said, "We've got some—"

"I'd like to hear from Keith now, Roy. Keith?"

Keith's eyes never left Wheeler's. "What the fuck are you doing on my property?"

Roy took a step forward. "Now Keith—"

Keith held a hand up to silence him. "I'll rephrase. What's your business, Wheeler?"

Wheeler grimaced in a look of exaggerated worry. "Still looking for those missing boys. You hear Dennis is missing, too?"

"I'd hardly call him a boy," Keith said. "And yeah, I heard."

"Know anything about that?"

"No."

The two men stared at each other in silence. Roy fidgeted in the background. He reminded Keith of a dog whose owners were arguing.

"Why are you here?" Keith said.

"I've just noticed that when left to your own devices, you tend to get into trouble. I figure it'd be good for you and the whole county if I came out and checked up on you every once in awhile. Especially with everything that's been going on."

"You checked. Now leave."

Wheeler slowly nodded. "Roy, you keep an eye on your brother here. He's got a hot head. And I've got this weird feeling I can't explain that says he's somehow involved in the bad things that have been going on recently."

"Now Bill–"

"Don't argue with me, Roy," Wheeler said. "Just keep a leash on him."

Wheeler turned and walked through the tall pasture grasses. Without turning back, he said, "I'll be around to check up on you again soon. Keep an eye out for Brandon and Dennis."

They watched him climb through the fence, get in his cruiser and drive away.

"Shit," Roy said. "What do we do now?"

Keith walked over to the coffin and knelt down. He ran his hand down the side. "Now we patch this here hole. Tonight I lock Brandon–I mean the vampire–in this shed. Tomorrow we go hunting for another vampire."

"Goddamn it Keith, you know what I mean! What about Bill?"

Keith looked over at him. Bill had certainly gotten Roy worked up. He looked about ready to pop.

"Roy, he's been nipping at my heels my whole life. He'll keep on nipping."

Roy took off his hat and wiped his brow with his shirtsleeve. "I don't know Keith. Maybe we should talk to him."

Without answering, Keith hauled his toolbox up onto the lid of the shed and started lining up the tools he needed to patch the gap in the wall.

CHAPTER 8

Dennis leaned against a small scrubby tree and watched Keith lead his best friend through the pasture. He could see Keith and Brandon as clearly as if it were daylight. More clearly even, at that distance. Keith gripped a chain attached to Brandon's collar tightly, but didn't pull it. Brandon scurried along behind him, docile as a house pet. As Keith led him along, Brandon looked all around and sniffed the air. He appeared to be starving for sensation. Dennis's anger rose and he pulled the branch he held off the tree.

Brandon heard this and looked straight at him. Keith didn't hear and couldn't see him in the dark, but Brandon could. Brandon shrieked and ran, hitting the end of the chain. Keith braced himself before he hit and held fast. He turned, slung the chain over his shoulder and plodded on, dragging Brandon behind him casual as could be. Eventually Brandon stopped fighting and let himself be guided into the strange wooden box. Keith shut the lid and locked it with two padlocks before returning to his house. He didn't look back over his shoulder even once.

What an over-confident idiot. He knew that monsters lurked in the darkness, and he still strutted around like a puffed-up rooster. Dennis wanted to kill him right then, but he didn't. He dropped the branch from his left hand. His bad hand. He hadn't gotten used to that yet. He held it in front of his face and flexed it, and dried blood fell away in flakes. He smiled, but the smile faded as he picked up his gas can and started toward Brandon's strange little prison.

He patted the wood. The thing was heavy-duty. He tugged lightly at the padlock's that secured two thick latches. Then he slid his clawed fingers under the edge of the lid and ripped it up, letting it clatter to the other side and hang from its hinges.

Brandon jumped to his feet. He stared at Dennis for a moment with huge black eyes, then leapt from the box and ran.

"Wait, Brandon," Dennis said as Brandon hit the end of his chain. His feet shot out from under him and he landed flat on his back, but he flipped into a crouch. He scrambled back and forth at the limit of the chain. Then he started batting at the chain with stumps that should have ended in hands, and Dennis felt sick to his stomach.

"Damn it, Brandon. Look what he's done to you." Dennis held his hands out, palms-forward. "Shhh... Shhh... It's alright. I know. I feel the same way. It's taking all my willpower to not either run away or kill you."

Dennis tried to get closer to Brandon, but Brandon scrambled in a circle, still attempting to remove his collar with hands that weren't there. Dennis shook his head as he stared into Brandon's eyes and saw no hint of recognition. He saw more than a lack of memory, but also a lack of human intelligence. It really was taking everything inside Dennis to be near Brandon. It must be even harder for

Brandon than it was for him, because Brandon was just an animal now. He'd hoped that somehow Brandon would have ended up like him. But that was just him grasping at anything from his old life. He'd lost his right-hand man. He was alone.

Dennis gave up walking after Brandon and sat on the edge of the box. "You were a loyal friend, and a good soldier. Yeah, I kind of blamed you for what happened to my arm, seeing as how you got Keith involved by sniffing around Jessica. But check this out." He worked his arm through an elaborate series of motions, showing Brandon how it was good as new. Then he chuckled and said, "So I guess no harm, no foul, huh?

"I'm sorry for locking you out of the van. I keep telling myself that I was already starting to lose it, but I don't know. I'm sorry. You saved me from that thing, and I don't know if I could have saved you. I could have tried. But I didn't know what the Hell was happening, you know? I didn't realize that I could save you.

"Whatever that bite put into my blood almost shut me down. It tried to do to my brain what it did to yours. I could barely think. So I just did what came natural, and it's sad to say, but what came natural was to put as much speed up my nose as I could. I just kept doing rail after rail, and eventually I felt myself die. The weird part is, I didn't mind."

He scraped his claws under his nose and down his mouth, pulling away flakes of blood.

"I came out of that van, and I knew that I had to eat. But I had to get away from Keith and the Sheriff. I smelled that fucking freak that attacked us and went after it. It was kind of like I was on auto-pilot. I just ran, mile after mile, going faster and faster, following that vampire. It knew I was coming, but so was the morning and it was weak, so it went to ground. Went back to its lair. I found it in this old abandoned barn, cowering under a sheet of old plywood in this shallow pit it'd dug out of the dirt floor."

Dennis smiled and shook his head. "You'd really put the hurt on it, man. It was beat all to Hell, just shaking there. I jumped on it, yanked its hair back and ripped its fucking throat out with my damn teeth. I didn't even know why. I know why now, but then, I was just doing what came natural. I drained it until it was nothing but a sack of bones and then I slept right there in its stinking pit."

Brandon had finally sat down at the end of his chain. When Dennis smiled, he cowered, and Dennis remembered his fangs. He supposed that vampires probably didn't really smile. "Anyway, the next day I felt so much stronger, so I've been hunting down more of the bloodsuckers. Draining them. Leaving them in the sun to burn up. When I feel another vampire out there, it takes all of my will to use that ability to hunt it instead of avoid it. But the blood leaves me so much stronger, not like the stuff you've been getting from cows. It's no wonder we're so territorial. Our blood is like crack and steroids rolled up in one delicious drink."

Dennis looked towards Keith's house and shook his head. "I'm gonna wipe the slate clean. This is my town now. Hell, my county. But there's one thing I have to do before that. I have to punish Keith Harris. I'm gonna take every good thing in his life and make it bad. By the time I get around to killing him, he'll beg me to do it."

He looked back to Brandon. "But I can't take you with me, man. Damn it, this really sucks."

Dennis hopped down, grabbed Brandon's chain and started reeling him in.

Brandon struggled wildly, hurling himself against the end of the chain. He'd lost some weight, but compared to

Dennis, he was still huge. Brandon's muscles rolled under his chalk-white skin as he flailed. But Dennis pulled him in like a leashed puppy. He marveled at how strong the vampire blood had made him.

"I didn't have any reason to hope, but I hoped you'd be like me. I can't take this alone. I'm going to have to make another vampire like myself."

Dennis grabbed Brandon's collar. He felt like he had to explain himself. "But even if you weren't just a dumb animal, look at what he's done to you. Look at your hands. I know how that feels. I don't think the real you would want to go on like this."

Brandon hissed in Dennis's face, and Dennis grimaced. "Your teeth... What kind of monster...?"

Dennis unlatched Brandon's collar.

Brandon felt at his neck with his stumps, and Dennis saw hope enter his eyes, and he felt horrible. Brandon turned and ran, but only got a few steps before Dennis jumped on his back, knocking him to his stomach. Dennis had undone the collar only because he needed access to Brandon's neck.

"I'm so sorry, Brandon," Dennis said. He crunched into Brandon's neck. The hunger took him then, and he didn't feel remorse again until he'd completely drained Brandon's filthy body.

When he finished, he stood. Blood that had already been clotting and rotting in Brandon's veins covered Dennis's face and chest and hands. He grabbed Brandon by an ankle and an arm, and hoisted him up into the box. Then he took his gas can and sloshed the fuel all over the box and Brandon.

"God, I hope you're not in there to feel this," Dennis said as he tossed in a match.

The box was transformed immediately from a prison to an enormous funeral pyre. Dennis roared along with the flames, and soon heard Keith's dogs barking from inside his house. He watched Keith emerge in boots and boxer shorts, holding a shotgun. Keith squinted toward the raging fire. Dennis doubted that Keith could see him at all.

"You're dead, old man," Dennis said. "But first, you've got some suffering to do."

CHAPTER 9

Keith watched Roy poke at the smoldering ruins of the box. Like Keith, he had a shotgun slung over his shoulder. Keith's dogs strained at their leashes, sniffing at the smell of vampires all around them.

The sun was only just rising, and the air was still cool.

"I can't find the bones. Are there bones after a vampire burns?" Roy asked.

"I don't know."

Roy tossed the stick aside and wiped the sweat from his face. He'd stirred up some red embers from beneath the gray ash. "I thought you said they were territorial. I thought you said our vampire would keep the others away."

"What the Hell do I know?"

Roy thought about it for a second, then said, "I always assume you know."

"I don't have anything to do with your assumptions," Keith said. He handed Roy a leash.

"What makes you say it was a vampire anyway?" Roy asked. "These things are dumb animals. How would it set a fire?"

"I heard it. It was a vampire."

"Then how did it do this?"

"Goddamn it Roy, I don't know!" Keith took a deep breath, then let it out. "I can't explain it. It screamed like a vampire, but it stood tall and watched me like a man."

Roy whistled, then looked confused. "You saw it all the way from your house?"

"It stood right in front of the fire. I could see its silhouette. It's like it wanted me to see it."

"We still going hunting?" Roy asked.

Keith nodded.

"We gonna try to find the one that did this?"

Keith nodded.

"We're gonna have to dig out the bones and bury them somewhere, if there are bones in there," Roy said.

"Should be cool enough by this afternoon. Let's go."

They started off in the direction the dogs were pulling. Roy broke off a stalk of straw and showed it to Keith. Dried blood. He walked another few steps and broke off another.

They followed the dogs through the pastures of tall, brittle grass. Every so often they came to a fence, lifted it for the dogs, then climbed through themselves. Every mile or so, depending on if they were headed straight in a cardinal direction, they crossed a dirt road. A few times they had to work their way through hedges of Osage orange trees, spiny with huge, slick thorns that tore at them. Keith found a shredded bit of cloth hanging from one as he attempted to work his own shirt loose. Finally, they entered denser trees on a downhill slope as they approached a creek.

The men walked carefully, their cowboy boots slipping down the bank of moist earth. The dogs tugged at their leashes until they made it into the creek where they splashed back and forth sniffing. Roy hesitated, but Keith carefully picked his way across the shallow creek and Roy followed.

The dogs tried to pick up the trail again on the other side but couldn't. They stalked back and forth with their noses snuffling the ground; first one sat down and began to whine, then the other. They looked at Keith for guidance.

Keith unhooked the leash from his hound's collar. "Let her loose," he said to Roy.

The dogs loped away, sniffing at the ground. They crossed and re-crossed the creek.

"This one is different," Roy said. "It meant to lose us."

Keith nodded. He watched the dogs run around for a bit, then began to walk along the bank towards an interesting looking tree. The creek had eroded the earth beneath it, exposing half its roots and creating a shallow cave. Keith crouched down and peered under the tree. It was dark and dank under there, even in the middle of the day. He grabbed a handful of soft, black soil and crumbled it between his fingers. It was extremely easy to dig into.

"Let's walk this creek. I've got a thought." Keith rinsed his hand in the shallow water, then whistled for the dogs. They came bounding up and he leashed them again.

The day had grown hot and Keith was grateful for the shade of the trees and the cool air that had settled down in the creek bed over the water. The dogs pulled ahead as he and Roy stumbled along over roots and slick rocks. After some time the dogs stopped and began baying at a particularly large, gnarled tree. Its roots nearly spanned the creek and were clogged with debris that had drifted downstream. The space beneath the tree where it overhung the bank was almost cavernous. The dogs continued to bay.

"Hush!" Keith said.

He dropped the leash and unslung his shotgun. He removed a small flashlight from his belt and aimed both beneath the tree, creeping slowly forward. As his eyes adjusted to the gloom he saw that in the furthest recesses fresh earth was scattered and piled.

"It stinks," Roy said. "You see it?"

"It's dug in."

"We going in after it?"

Keith wondered about his brother's trust in him. It seemed infinite. Roy would follow Keith through the gates of Hell and feel perfectly safe as long as Keith said he was. That often felt like more responsibility than Keith wished to have.

Keith knew where that trust came from. Keith had always protected Roy, from bullies, from tough decisions. And when they were young, getting into boyish mischief, Keith always caught it double from their father, first for doing wrong himself, second for dragging Roy into it. All while Roy hid safe in their mother's apron.

"I'm not getting that close. We'll come back this evening. Get it as it comes out."

"You think this is the one that started the fire?"

"Guess so."

Roy nodded, then looked around. "Where are we, anyway?"

Keith grabbed his dog's leash and motioned for Roy to follow him up the bank. Once they emerged from the trees, Keith pointed across the pasture to a big, shiny red barn.

"This is the Irving's property," Roy said. "Let's cut across to the road."

Keith nodded, and they began walking through the tall grass.

Back in Keith's pasture, the brothers sifted through ashes with heavy rakes. Four concrete plugs with the scorched ends of four-by-fours projecting out of them marked the corners of the consumed shed. They were both covered in soot from head to boots, and each wore goggles over his eyes and a bandana over his mouth.

It turned out that there were bones left in the pile, but that they burned up in a flash when they were exposed to sunlight. So they raked through the ashes again and again, spreading the pile further out, occasionally getting a pop like a flashbulb when they uncovered a new bone. But that happened less and less.

"You finding anymore bones?" Roy asked.

"Nope."

"Guess we must have got them all."

"Saw the smoke this morning."

Keith spun around. Sheriff Wheeler was approaching from the direction of the gravel road.

"Oh shit," Roy whispered from behind his bandana.

"Keep your mouth shut," Keith hissed.

Wheeler didn't seem to have heard them. "With all the weird shit going on, you two barely make the cut." He smiled. "So what happened here?"

"Don't know."

"Someone committed arson on your property and you didn't contact us?"

Keith didn't say anything. He just took off his goggles and pulled down his bandana.

"You two look like a couple of bandits with those things on. Almost makes me suspicious."

"Maybe he did it himself, accidentally," Roy said. "So why are you here?"

Wheeler frowned, and not sarcastically. "I expect that attitude from your brother, but not you, Roy. You know the saying 'where there's smoke, there's fire?' Well right now, those ashes aren't so interesting. But you're certainly smoking, Roy."

Keith had had enough of Wheeler to last him the rest of his life. Wheeler seemed to think he had something on Keith, something that would keep Keith careful. He was wrong.

Roy started to speak, when Keith put a hand on his chest and stepped forward. "We've got this under control, Bill. So how about you leave?"

"I don't know if it really looks like you—"

"How about you leave while you still can?"

Sheriff Wheeler rested his hand on the butt of his holstered revolver. "Is that a threat?"

Keith nodded at the gun. "You think that'll even things up? We know who the better man is, and it's by a might bit bigger difference than that makes."

"We know the better man, huh?"

Keith spit at Wheeler's boots. "Irene settled that."

Sheriff Wheeler began to square up, and so did Keith, but Roy stepped between them.

"Please go, Sheriff. We're doing nothing wrong."

The two tall men stared at each other for a long while, but eventually Wheeler backed away.

"I'll be back to check on you boys again soon. And Roy, next time you better keep a tighter hold on his leash."

Keith stared after Sheriff Wheeler as he walked away. He didn't think that Wheeler was actually dumb enough to come poking around again anytime soon. Keith would love to put that bastard in the ground regardless of the consequences. He figured that was the biggest difference between himself and Bill. Neither of them had much to lose, but Bill seemed to care anyway.

"Good Lord that was close," Roy said. "That was so close. Why'd you have to bring up Irene?"

"Was sick of his game. Sick of the talk." Keith looked at Roy. Roy's hands shook, but he clenched his rake hard when he saw Keith notice. Keith patted his shoulder. "You go on home and clean up. Come 'round my place at seven."

Roy looked at the ashes, "You sure you don't need help?"

"No. Go on."

"Alright. See you at seven."

Keith sat on his porch, still covered in soot. He sipped from the beer in his hand. He looked at his watch. One. There were too many hours between one and seven. He was too worked up to do anything but sit there and drink his beer. He drained it, then went to the kitchen for another. The snake skull sat atop his fridge, and he stared into its hollow eyes. He grabbed the bourbon beside it. It was a liter bottle, about half full from the last time. He took it outside with him.

Sitting in the chair he chased slugs of bourbon with gulps of beer, and he remembered the day he buried Irene.

He remembered standing beside the fresh grave with Pastor Conway. He and the Pastor stayed as the others wandered away a few at a time. But when Keith looked up from the casket, Sheriff Wheeler and Deputy Thomas stood opposite him. The deputy whispered to Wheeler, but kept glancing at Keith. When he saw Keith notice them, he talked faster and tried to move Wheeler away, but Wheeler glared at Keith. He shrugged off the big man's hand and stalked around the grave.

"Seeing you here like this—"

"Sheriff, please," the deputy said, trying to press himself between them.

"–I can't help but say something," Wheeler continued.

Keith looked at him and waited for the man to give him an excuse.

"Sheriff, have some decency," Pastor Conway said.

"You already questioned him," Deputy Thomas said.

But Keith didn't hear them. He waited. Waited for Wheeler to give him a reason.

Wheeler didn't seem to hear them either. He said, "Eighteen years ago, she chose you. And it was the wrong choice."

"Sheriff!" Deputy Thomas said.

"Let me say my piece. I always knew there was something wrong with you, but I thought that she had you under control. I figure she must have thought so, too. But we were wrong. And because I made that mistake, she's dead."

The Sheriff stepped closer, and Keith waited.

"You're not a man. You're a rabid animal. You need to be put down. And I'm going to prove it. And I'm going to do it."

Keith waited.

"I know it was you. It wasn't equipment malfunction. You murdered her you–"

Keith punched Wheeler across his jaw and Wheeler dropped to the ground. The big deputy tried to grab Keith, but Keith shoved him into the open grave and onto Irene's casket. Keith sat on Wheeler and hit him again and again until Pastor Conway, who was no small man, dragged him off. Keith managed to stomp his boot into Wheeler's face once before he was restrained.

CHAPTER 10

Even though she'd chided him for his hermit-like ways, Jessica felt guilty about not visiting her uncle more often. She liked him. She knew that uncles got to be the fun ones, but it wasn't just that. Sometimes she felt more similar to him than to her own father. She wouldn't ever tell her dad, but she respected Keith more.

And Keith needed her. He and Irene had always enjoyed having her around. She guessed it was because they didn't have any kids of their own. And now that Irene was gone, she felt like he needed her to keep him from disappearing inside himself.

So after her dad came back curiously filthy from "hunting" with her uncle, she dug through her clothes until she found her keys and headed down the road.

She knew she'd find him on his porch, and there he sat, sleeping in his chair when she pulled up. But he didn't wake up when she got out and slammed her car door. She saw the cans of beer and the mostly-empty bottle of bourbon lying on its side.

Jessica walked up the steps and patted Keith on the shoulder.

"Keith."

When he didn't respond, she shook him a bit. "Keith! Uncle Keith!"

He muttered but didn't wake up. God, it had probably only been an hour since her dad left him, and he was already passed-out drunk. She hated to get in other peoples' business, especially with the problems she'd had, but she really might have to talk to him about his drinking. She'd heard her parents worrying about how bad he'd gotten. What had finally shaken her out of her stupid rebellious stage was when she understood how much she was hurting the people who cared about her and compared that to how little she got from the drugs and the partying.

She sighed and picked up the bottle of bourbon. A little bit of amber liquid sloshed in the bottom. She took a small swig and scrunched her face and shook her head. She usually drank beer, and when she drank liquor, she mixed.

Jessica gathered up the empty cans of beer and awkwardly opened the screen door. She dropped the cans in the trash, dumped the bit of bourbon into the sink, then dropped the bottle into the trash, too. Then she opened the fridge.

Nothing but beer. The man lived on alcohol and junk food. She'd definitely have to talk to him.

She grabbed a can, opened it, and sipped as she looked at the pictures on the fridge. There were a few pictures of her as a little girl, and a few pictures of Keith and Irene. She slipped one of those pictures out from beneath a magnet.

Jessica had been young enough when Irene died that she didn't miss her too much, except for Keith's sake. But she remembered Irene as being tough with the men but very kind to her. Irene taught her how to play Pitch, and then let her be her partner. She was so good that they always won, even when Jessica made mistakes, as a little kid would.

As Jessica replaced the photo beneath its magnet, she noticed the rattlesnake skull sitting atop the fridge. It seemed to menace her with its fangs. They seemed to reach out to her. She almost picked it up, but hesitated and finally withdrew her hand without touching it.

Back outside she sat on the porch rail.

"Keith."

Keith continued to sleep in his chair. She finished off her beer and sat it on the rail. Then she picked Keith's cowboy hat up off the porch and set it over his face to protect it from the western sun.

CHAPTER 11

"Keith," Roy said. "Keith!"

Keith sat up, his hat falling from his face. "Huh?"

"Jessica said you were passed-out drunk. What kind of example are you setting?"

Keith held his head in his hands. He could feel his heart pounding just behind his eyes, trying to crack his skull open. "Jessica was here?"

"Yeah, she said she tried to wake you up for a few minutes. She said she'd promised to visit more often. So what's the point if you're going to be unconscious?"

"Was she angry?"

"No. She acted like she thought it was funny, though I think she's worried. *I'm* angry. And aren't we supposed to go? You look terrible."

Roy had showered and put on clean clothes.

Keith pressed himself up out of his chair. He felt a bit wobbly, but tried to hide it.

"I'm fine."

"You don't look—"

"I said I'm fine!" Roy jumped a bit and Keith felt bad. He knew he deserved some dressing-down. "I just need some water."

"I bet you do," Roy said. "How much did you drink?"

"I don't remember," Keith said. "All of it, I guess."

"All of it," Roy said. He stifled a laugh. "Well, chug down some water and get your gear. The sun's gonna set soon."

Roy was right. The sun sat low in the sky, almost touching the horizon.

Keith parked his truck beside the Irvings' property. He and Roy jogged across their pasture toward the creek. They slid down the bank and sloshed through the water. The going was far more difficult in the dark, but they made it and settled down behind some brush across from the big strange tree.

Keith brought his shotgun to bear on the dark cavern beneath the tree.

"Do you think we're too late?" Roy asked.

"No."

"It's dark with all these trees. Can't tell where the sun's at."

Keith hushed him.

It was dark. Keith held a flashlight against the shotgun, but didn't know if it would be enough.

Keith heard the vampire moving before he saw it. The soft earth it shoved aside made only a soft sound. Keith nodded to Roy, and Roy nodded back.

The vampire's white flesh caught the little moonlight that strained down through the canopy. Still, it was just an undefined gray smudge in the dark. Keith tried to get a shot, but it scuttled through the heavy root system. Then he heard a light snuffling sound. Then a shriek.

The vampire burst from beneath the tree and raced up the bank. Keith flipped the flashlight on with his thumb and tried to draw a bead on the vampire. It tore at the ground and the trees with its hands as it ran, hurtling itself from side to side and steadily up. All of Keith's concentration went to trying to predict where the thing would step next, when the night suddenly exploded, and so did the vampire's head.

Roy had taken the shot. The vampire lay twitching on the opposite bank.

"Goddamn it, Roy!"

"What?"

They scrambled across the creek. The headless vampire's limbs still moved. Its clawed hands flexed spasmodically.

"You blew its head clean off," Keith said.

"Sorry."

"I told you to aim for the body."

"I'm sorry! It surprised me, okay? I didn't expect it to move that fast."

Keith dragged his eyes away from the vampire and looked at Roy. Roy's eyes were huge. Keith chuckled. "It sure did move. Must've smelled us."

Roy forced out a laugh. "Moved like a big spider. You think it'll heal?"

Keith looked at the body. Its twitching was subsiding.

"No."

"Brandon healed."

"I'm betting it needs its head to heal."

Roy nodded. "That makes sense." He poked at the vampire's foot with his boot. "So what do we do with it?"

Keith and Roy stood in the back of Keith's truck. Keith held the vampire beneath its armpits. Roy held its ankles.

Keith counted as they swung it back and forth, then chucked it onto the charred remains of Brandon's shed.

The vampire's limbs and joints seemed looser than a human's. It lay atop the ashes in a twisted pile. Keith tossed the largest chunks of its head beside it. He'd gathered up the bits that seemed identifiable as human in case anyone came to check on the gunshot. They wouldn't, but still.

"Maybe we should have re-buried it under the tree," Roy said.

"It stinks too bad. Someone would have found it."

"I know. I just want to be done with the thing."

"We're nowhere near done."

Roy sighed. "I know." He looked Keith up and down. "You okay? You look like crap."

"Thanks," Keith said. "I'll be fine."

Roy hopped out of the back of Keith's pickup. He climbed through the fence and started towards across the pasture towards his own house, but stopped and turned back. "Hey, you want to go to church with us in the morning?"

"Tomorrow's Sunday?"

Roy laughed. "Yeah."

"No."

"I just thought... We've talked more in the past couple days than the past couple years. So I thought maybe... Nevermind. See you after church."

Roy started for his house again. Keith opened his mouth to say something, but he didn't know what he'd say, so he shut it again.

CHAPTER 12

Dennis examined the cone of brains, blood and bits of skull sprayed out from where the vampire had fallen, and smiled. Yes, he'd wanted to eat that vampire himself, but he decided to offer it to Keith as a scapegoat.

He knelt where the corpse had leaked out a pool of blood onto the grass and dipped his fingers into it. The brothers hadn't been gone long, but the blood was already tacky. He licked his fingers, then scooped up more. He couldn't help it.

He stopped himself just short of licking the ground and stood. That's when he noticed the Irvings' big dairy barn.

He'd driven past it plenty of times back when he was alive. It stood out. For one thing, it was really big. For another, it was modern looking, all made of metal. This wasn't one of the collapsing heaps that stood on most of these old boys' properties, a more scenic version of a car on cinderblocks. No, the Irvings had the biggest dairy operation in the area, and they had a serious barn to match. And something about it sparked Dennis's imagination.

He crossed the pasture in no time and slid the barn's big metal track door open. He could see just fine, but he flipped the light switch. Down the central aisle, a row of suspended fluorescent lights buzzed to life one by one.

Dennis had never seen the inside of the barn. It was even more modern than the exterior. The floors were concrete, not dirt, with a channel for mucking the stalls running down each side of the aisle. Dennis could see that the channels could be flushed almost like a toilet.

The milking stalls were all high-tech, too. Dennis had heard that happy cows made more milk, and he thought that these were probably some happy, milky cows. He walked down the aisle, running his claws along the steel bars. Then he found a big coil of rope and smiled.

Matthew and Rachel Irving were good, God-fearing, hardworking folk, so Dennis had never spoken to them. Whenever he'd happened to be in their vicinity—at the convenience store or at a ball game—they always acted like he was stinking up the place. He'd never done anything to them. He'd never gone out of his way to intimidate them or make them feel uncomfortable. And still they acted so superior that they intimidated him. They went out of their way to make him uncomfortable.

So he found it very satisfying on a personal level to kick in their back door.

He was already standing at the foot of their bed when Matt Irving said, "Rachel?"

"What was that?" Rachel said.

Matt sat up. "I don't know." He flipped on the bedside lamp.

Dennis smiled at them, grabbed them each by an ankle, and dragged them out of the house. He felt better and better about himself as they flailed around and screamed and he pulled them down stairs and around corners and over wood and rock and finally concrete and tossed them into neighboring stalls.

He bound their wrists and ankles with rope and tied them to the stainless steel bars. Rachel sobbed silently. Dennis liked that. Matthew sat with his eyes clamped shut and his jaw set in impotent rage. Dennis liked that even more. He leaned on the gates of their stalls and admired them.

"Dennis, why are you doing this? What have we ever done to you?" Rachel said. She hiccupped between words, and tears streamed down her pudgy cheeks.

He could tell them. He could describe how it felt to be snubbed for no reason by a whole town. But he didn't want to give them the satisfaction. And they would never be able to make him feel small again, anyway. No one would.

"You never did anything to me," he said. "Don't take this personal."

"Then why are you doing this? What do you want?"

"Rachel," Matthew Irving barked.

Dennis liked that Matthew seemed to feel that he still had some amount of control. He would enjoy taking that away from him.

"I've been inspired by your setup here: your barn, your cows. I used to think you ranchers were a bunch of ignorant hicks. Now I see the truth. You're higher on the food chain, so you keep those lower on the food chain close to hand. You never worry about going hungry. That really inspired me. Only an idiot goes hunting every night when he can keep his meals leashed up."

"I don't understand," Rachel said. "Is this about drugs? What are you talking about?

"The natural order," Dennis said. "And you happen to be lower on the food chain. So like I said, it's nothing personal. You're just the first cattle in my herd.

"But Matt," Dennis said. "Just because you raise cows doesn't mean you have to fuck one! No offense Rachel." He laughed.

"How high are you?" Matthew said.

"Matthew!" Rachel said, but Matthew kept going.

"What are you on? Even you aren't usually this incoherent."

Dennis spoke at the same time, almost to himself. "All I hear is 'moo.'"

"Sheriff Wheeler is going to have a field day with you."

"All I hear is 'eat me.'"

"Matthew, stop antagonizing him," Rachel said through her panicked sobs and gasps.

Dennis jumped the gate to Matthew's stall and began to close in, and smiled. And showed his mouthful of fangs. Finally, Dennis saw the hard man break, he saw the sense of superiority meet with reality, and it was the best high he'd ever felt.

"Stay away from me!"

"All I hear is, 'I am fat and juicy and fit for slaughter.'"

Dennis pinned Matthew Irving to the stall with one hand. The fear, the promise of the kill, it was taking over. He felt his human side slipping away, and he let it go. As if entranced, he said, "All I hear is your beating heart and rushing blood."

He ripped out Matthew's throat. He'd intended to keep his cattle alive, but he lost his self-restraint at that moment. He drank his fill.

Logan had always annoyed the shit out of Dennis. Dennis guessed the rancher figured he was old and senile enough that he could get away with saying whatever he wanted, and more than once he'd told Dennis what he thought of him. And Logan didn't think too highly of him.

He owned the property north of the Irvings' place.

Through the big picture window, Dennis saw the old coot kicked back in his recliner watching TV. It was a pitiful sight. Honestly, it would be a mercy to put the bastard out of his misery. Dennis knocked on the door, the upper-half of which was composed of nine small panes of glass. When Logan peered through the glass, Dennis just reached through and yanked him out. But he was surprised when Mandy Logan came running into the front room from the kitchen.

Mandy was the old man's granddaughter. She must have been home for the weekend from Lawrence, where she went to KU. Dennis didn't know her well, but thought she must be some sort of saint for visiting that angry old fart on a Saturday night. He grabbed her, too.

Dennis sat on top of the QuickStop. The night was beautiful. He'd always been a night person, which was good, considering his profession, but he'd never really experienced the night like he had since his change. He could see and hear everything around him so clearly. He could practically hear the stars humming.

Dennis was happy with his small herd, but knew he'd accelerated things considerably. It was important that he be prepared to deal with Keith, and for that he needed Patty Seller. Patty had worked at the QuickStop for years. She'd worked there part-time in high school, and for the past few years, she had worked their full-time. She was a cutie, thin with long legs and long hair. She had a big nose, but the rest of her made up for it. And she'd always been nice to Dennis. Roger, who owned the QuickStop, hated Dennis, of course, but Patty seemed to like him. She'd chat him up when he came in to buy something, and never got on him about hanging around. He'd come real close to asking her out on a few different occasions. But some of the kids called her Patty Smeller because of her nose, and he didn't want to have to deal with that.

At midnight, he heard her lock the front doors. A minute later she walked out the side door by the dumpster, where she always parked her old Chevy S-10 pickup. Dennis fell on her from above. He felt some bones snap, but she was still conscious and struggling. He wrapped his fingers in her hair and smacked her face into the concrete twice. Holding her up by her hair, he looked her face over. Her nose was smashed flat and blood ran from her forehead. That would do.

Dennis dropped her into the back of her pickup and drove off. A couple of miles outside of town he felt the shocks bounce and looked back to see Patty roll herself over the side of the truck bed. She managed to hit the grass shoulder, but she was still unconscious from the impact when he put her in the passenger seat. He couldn't believe she was still alive. He wouldn't have thought it to look at her, but she was tough.

After securing Patty in her own stall, Dennis's final stop of the night was Roy's house. It was one in the morning by the time he made it over there. He didn't see any lights on, but he didn't want to circle the house for fear of waking the dogs. Instead, he walked straight up and stood beneath an open second-floor window and sniffed. Jessica. He took a few steps back and got a running start, then jumped, grabbed the window sill, and slid into the room in one fluid movement.

Jessica didn't stir in her sleep.

Her room was a mess. The floor was covered in clothes and magazines. Dennis smiled at the angry posters on the walls and the stuffed animals in the corners. He remembered being that age, when he'd worshipped heavy metal bands but didn't want to give up his action figures.

He stepped closer to the bed. Asleep, she looked younger than usual. Especially because she was normally scowling at him when he saw her. With her face slack, he could see more of the little girl and less of the sharp Harris bone structure. He wondered which features would become more prominent after he'd changed her.

But after watching her for a few moments, Dennis slid back out the window. That question would be answered another night.

CHAPTER 13

Sheriff Wheeler stood beside Pastor Conway in the doorway of the small church. The congregation flowed slowly inside, and the two men chatted between greetings. The Pastor wanted to talk about the recent activity with the cattle, and about the missing men. Wheeler didn't want to discuss any of that. He felt glad to be coming together with his happy community at church on a sunny Sunday. He watched them greet each other and chat on the lawn. His work could get him down. It never ended. The animal nature of some people wouldn't let it. But seeing those he kept safe all together like that made it worth it.

"Guys like that just get up and leave. That's what they do. They don't have the same ties we do," Wheeler said to the Pastor.

"You really think that's what happened?"

"Most likely." He didn't think that at all, but that was the answer that would end the conversation.

Roy approached with his wife Sheila and their daughter Jessica. Wheeler smiled when he saw Jessica. She looked very pretty in a floral print dress, but apparently refused to remove her many bracelets and necklaces. She'd fallen in with the wrong crowd for a bit, but she seemed to have gotten herself straightened out, and Wheeler guessed she'd be headed off to college after her senior year.

"Hello, Sheriff. Pastor Conway," Roy said. He smiled a bit bashfully.

"Hey there, Roy," Wheeler said with a bit of extra good will in his voice. He slapped Roy on the back to show he held no grudge. "How'd an ugly fella like you end up with these lovely ladies?"

Wheeler and the Pastor had just started talking again when Doris, the church secretary, came out of the church and joined them on the stoop.

"Pastor Conway, Rachel Irving isn't here."

"Do you know where she is?"

"No, she isn't answering her phone."

"I don't think she's ever missed a service before." Rachel always played the organ.

"I've been trying to get a hold of her," Doris said.

"I suppose we'll just have to start without her. See you after the service, Bill."

Pastor Conway walked straight up to the pulpit as Wheeler took the seat Deputy Thomas had saved for him with his family.

"Many of you have probably noticed the absence of Rachel's beautiful music," Pastor Conway began. "She is unable to join us today, so we'll have to make do. Let us begin."

They started with prayers that Wheeler knew so well he barely noticed them anymore, then sang a hymn. Rachel's absence from her place at the organ became conspicuous. Then the pastor began his sermon.

"Today I would like to talk to you about the burden of sin we all bear. We each carry a heavy load in our souls. Sometimes, it can wear us down. Sometimes, it seems like too much to carry. But as Psalm 32 shows us, when we turn to the Lord, we can find relief from that burden. Please read with me."

Wheeler read along, but he watched Roy Harris. Wheeler could never fault a man for being loyal to his brother, but he sincerely hoped that Roy managed to stay out of whatever disaster Keith was working to bring down upon himself. Roy was a good man, and he had a family to care for.

After they read the psalm, Pastor Conway said, "Sometimes, we can't help but wonder why evil profits in this life. Sometimes, it's hard to wait for our reward in the afterlife as we suffer in this life. But know that evil never truly profits, in this world or the next. Sometimes it may seem that it does, but know that while we feel light of soul when we turn to the Lord, the wicked feel the full weight of their burden. They are crushed under every ounce of it."

Wheeler wondered if that were true. He worked to preserve the law, and tried to ensure that evil didn't prosper in this world, but it obviously did. He was no idiot. But was there a lightness of soul that one couldn't pay for, and a weight of sin that couldn't be bought off? It seemed mean-spirited, but he hoped so. And he hoped that Keith felt the crush of his sins every moment of every day.

CHAPTER 14

Sitting on his porch, a beer in his hand, Keith wore the same soot-covered clothes on Sunday that he had on Saturday. Roy pulled up in his truck and got out wearing his church clothes.

"Don't look at me like that," Keith said.

"Like what?"

Keith pointed to Roy's face. He killed the beer and popped open another.

"A little hair of the dog that bit you?" Roy asked.

Keith nodded.

"Actually, I'm not sure it's hair of the dog if you never stopped drinking."

Keith shrugged. "You here in your Sunday best to talk about my drinking?"

"No. We need to, but that's not why I'm here today."

Keith nodded, drinking his beer. He felt his fuse burning already. Even he was surprised by how short it had gotten.

"It was the sermon this morning," Roy said. "I wish you would have come to church and heard it."

"I sense a sermon coming on, regardless."

"Well, you should have heard Pastor Conway give it. It was about our burden of sin."

Roy looked like he was waiting for a response, but it was all Keith could do to keep his mouth shut. Roy usually didn't push Keith to the snapping point. He usually knew just when to stop. But Keith didn't think he'd stop this time.

"I've been feeling this burden real bad, but I didn't understand it until I heard Pastor Conway describe it. First of all, these things were people."

"Emphasis on were."

"That's what I said. And that's bad enough. These were people, and I blew one's head off."

Keith chuckled, remembering the frantic confusion of that moment.

"It's not funny! And regardless of what you think about whether or not these vampires are still people, they're definitely killing people. They were all human once. So every day we don't tell someone what we know is a day someone else might be getting turned into one of them monsters."

Roy paused. Keith sipped his beer.

"I can't take it anymore," Roy said. "I feel like I'm dragging around an anchor. I'm telling Sheriff Wheeler."

"Hell you are," Keith said. He snorted. "Wheeler."

"I'm telling Sheriff Wheeler so he can tell the proper authorities."

"They'll take everything," Keith said. "They'll–"

"It doesn't make sense anymore! Somehow it made sense once, but it doesn't now."

Keith stopped and breathed, so that he wouldn't shout. So that he wouldn't get to his feet. So that what always followed when he got to his feet wouldn't happen. "It doesn't have to make sense to you, Roy. You just have to do what you're told."

"Goddamn it, Keith!"

"Yell all you like. You're not telling anybody." Keith killed that beer and popped another. Warm like that, they went down fast.

"I'm a grown fucking man."

Keith looked at his little brother standing there in his church clothes, cursing and throwing a tantrum. "You're not telling anybody."

"Or what?'

And Keith stood up. "I shouldn't need to say what."

Roy stared Keith in the eyes. Keith gave him that. But he was bigger than Roy. He was stronger than Roy. And most of all, he knew that what Roy saw living behind his eyes was of a species completely different from what lived inside Roy. And Roy didn't even know he was holding it back.

So inevitably, Roy walked down the porch stairs. He spoke with his back to Keith.

"Fine then. Fine. I'd tell you that all the consequences will be on your head, but I don't think you'd care. But don't put a vampire anywhere near my property. I want nothing more to do with this. And I won't be coming around if you've got a vampire over here."

Roy headed for his truck. Then Keith thought of something.

"What about Jessica?"

Roy climbed in his truck and Keith went to the edge of the porch.

"What about Jessica?" Keith asked again.

"I don't know."

Roy drove away. Keith sat back down. He vibrated with something like rage and sorrow and he didn't know what it all was. And he didn't know why he couldn't stop.

Roy be goddamned. What did he know about burdens? Sheltered little mama's boy.

He didn't think Keith felt the weight of consequences?

Keith knew about burdens. Keith remembered Irene, laying in her hospital bed. So tiny. So tired.

He asked, "How can you ask me to do that?"

"I'm not asking you to do it. I'm just asking you to get it. Just bring it to me."

"How can you ask me to be a part of this? How could I live with myself?" She was nothing like Irene. She didn't even look like Irene. And his wife would never have asked him to do what she was asking.

She said, "Keith, please! The doctors said it could take months. I can't take months. They've given up on me. I'm here to die. Why should I wait in pain?"

"Because..." His mouth worked, but nothing came out.

"Nevermind. I know why. I'm sorry. I didn't mean it."

He wouldn't look at her. He was failing her.

"Come here, Keith. I said I'm sorry."

Keith went inside and into his pantry. He grabbed one of the four handle bottles of bourbon inside. He kept the stash for days like this, Sundays like this, when they wouldn't sell you alcohol. What did the state of Kansas expect people like him to do on Sundays? Kill themselves, he guessed.

CHAPTER 15

Sheriff Wheeler lived in a ranch house on a few acres just outside of town. He called it his country-boy bachelor pad. His hunting and fishing trophies covered the wood-paneled walls. His huge, overstuffed leather furniture faced his big-screen television. When a guy didn't have a wife and kids, a Sheriff's salary went pretty far. He even had a pool table.

Wheeler sat in the middle of his couch, eating dinner off a tray and watching TV. The telephone rang. He looked at it and sighed. He knew from many attempts that he could not reach the side table on which the telephone sat from the middle of the couch with a tray of food over his legs. He moved the tray, being careful not to tip it and spill his bottle of beer, and answered the phone.

"Bill Wheeler speaking."

"Sheriff, this is Tom Conway."

"What can I do for you, Pastor?"

"I'm a bit worried about the Irvings."

Wheeler had forgotten that they weren't at church. "Is anything the matter?"

"I don't know that anything is the matter, but I still haven't heard from them. I stopped by their place when I had a minute and no one answered the door."

"Maybe they went on a trip. Family got sick or something."

"Rachel wouldn't leave without telling me she wouldn't be able to play for the service."

"I see what you're saying. I'm not on duty right now, but if you call the office, one of my deputies will check on them."

"But I don't know that anything's wrong."

Wheeler accepted that he wasn't going to get out of checking on them. "I'm sure they're fine, but I'll go take a look."

"I'd feel much better. Thank you, Sheriff."

"No problem, Pastor. You have to look out for your flock."

Wheeler knocked on the Irvings' front door. No one answered. He stepped back and looked up at the two-story farm house. Everything looked okay. But it probably would.

In the back of his mind, he noted cattle lowing. A lot of them.

He walked around the house. The side windows were too high to peek into. When he reached the back of the house, he drew his gun. The backdoor stood wide open, the frame splintered at the latch.

Wheeler stepped quietly through the utility room on the back porch, holding his gun and his flashlight before him. As he made his way through the kitchen and dining room and into the foyer, he noticed that some things were in disarray while others were untouched. It didn't look as if they'd been robbed, but there was a table pulled out of place, a chair knocked over, a bunch of books pulled from the bookshelf.

He made his way up the stairs. It was one of the rare times that he wished he wore normal shoes instead of cowboy boots. Since he couldn't help but make noise anyway, he said, "Matthew? Rachel? It's Sheriff Wheeler."

There was no reply.

In the bedroom the situation became clearer. There he found the real evidence of a struggle. Blankets were torn from the bed and trailed to the doorway. One piece of door trim had been yanked off the wall, and when he looked closely at a bloody place on the ground, he found fingernails peeled off between the floorboards.

He followed the trail back out. It looked as if several men had abducted the Irvings, literally dragging them from their bed. He could almost see them grabbing at chairs and books as they were pulled along.

He hadn't noticed it before, but the trail extended out from the back door. A worn dirt path went from the door toward the barn. Now he saw gouges where fingers had raked at the earth. He saw blood.

Wheeler jogged to the barn and found the noisy cattle. The barn interrupted a barbed wire fence, with the back door opening into a pasture. The cows stood along the other side of the fence, waiting to be milked. So the Irvings hadn't been there that morning to milk them. Wheeler reached for the handle of the huge metal sliding door and found that it was coated in dried blood. He slid the door open and aimed the flashlight inside, but the barn was so large that the beam only illuminated dust in the air. Taking one step inside the door, Wheeler aimed his gun forward in his right hand, and searched for a light switch with his left. It took him a minute to find and flip the switch. Just as he did something grabbed his wrist and squeezed hard. The gun fell from Wheeler's hand.

"Dennis?"

"Yes, Sheriff." Dennis smiled and squeezed harder. Wheeler felt his wrist bones grind together and fell to his knees groaning.

Dennis dragged him down the aisle of stalls. Through squinted, tear-filled eyes, Wheeler saw Dennis's prisoners, bound and bleeding. They watched him with wide eyes.

"My God..." he said, just before Dennis flung him into a stall. His head smacked the concrete and everything went black.

CHAPTER 16

Keith lay snoring on top of the comforters, still wearing the same, dirty clothes. Beer cans littered the floor. The dogs began barking from the utility room, but it wasn't enough to wake Keith. Besides, it was only a second later that Dennis leapt through Keith's bedroom door and onto the bed, pinning Keith's shoulders with his knees.

Keith jerked his head up and struggled to move. "What? What the...?"

Dennis smiled down at him and let him struggle. Eventually, Keith understood what was happening and stopped. It wasn't doing any good, only giving Dennis satisfaction.

Dennis leaned over and flipped on the bedside lamp. His knee crushed Keith's shoulder. Keith worked to conceal the grimace.

"You're not looking good, Keith. I think you're losing it."

"You don't look so great yourself."

Dennis ran his clawed, blood coated hands down his shirt. The stiff fabric didn't respond to the tidying movement. "You don't seem surprised to see me." He smiled, displaying his fangs.

"I figured the vampires got you, being a scrawny little cripple. Knew it was you must have killed Brandon. You always seemed jealous of him."

Dennis stopped smiling. "That's not true. He couldn't go on after what you'd done to him, you sick bastard." Dennis regained his composure and smiled again. "Things kinda got flipped, now. You made me a cripple, but I ain't crippled anymore. And look at you. The big tough rancher pinned like a bug."

Dennis grabbed Keith's face and leaned forward, baring his fangs. He moved Keith's head around, making him examine the changes he'd undergone.

Dennis was acting like a big man, like he'd always tried to do.

While he fooled around, Keith worked his right hand down into his pocket. Dennis had his arm pinned down by his side, but he managed to pull out his pocketknife.

"Don't worry," Dennis said. "I'm not gonna kill you yet. Before I'm done with you, you'll beg for my fangs."

"Course you're not gonna kill me." Keith flicked the knife open and jammed it into the back of Dennis's thigh. Dennis screamed and fell backwards off Keith's chest, onto his butt on the bed. Keith sat up, slammed the knife into Dennis's throat and pulled it from ear to ear.

Black, clotted blood poured from the huge wound. Dennis held it with both hands and rolled off the bed. He stumbled for the door, but Keith followed after him, stabbing him in the back over and over, aiming for the lungs and kidneys with the stout blade.

Dennis fell to his knees and crawled for the stairs, still gripping his slit throat with one hand.

"I thought you were some kind of badass now," Keith said. He kicked Dennis, sending him rolling down the stairs.

At the landing, Dennis managed to get to his hands and knees.

"No," he croaked. He turned and faced Keith, and rose up from his hands into a kneeling position. Keith watched the wound in Dennis's throat seal itself up, closing from the outside edges to the center, until it was completely healed. Dennis shouted, "No!"

From the top of the stairs, Keith whipped the knife. It thunked solidly into Dennis's forehead. Dennis fell backward with his legs twisted awkwardly beneath him and stared blankly up at the ceiling. He was motionless except for his hands, which fluttered on his limp wrists like wounded birds.

Keith snorted and sat on the top step, breathing hard.

Then Dennis reached up and pulled the knife from his skull.

"Goddamn it," Keith said.

Dennis rolled over and got to his hands and knees. Keith ran down the stairs and kicked him in the stomach several times, but Dennis rose shakily. Keith hit Dennis in the jaw as he got to his feet, until Dennis stood before him. Keith stopped hitting him when he saw that Dennis was letting him do it.

Dennis flexed his jaw and wiggled it in his hand. Then he smiled and nodded. "You ever box?"

Keith glowered at him.

Dennis shoved Keith with both hands, sending him flying. His back hit the wall, then his head, and for a second his vision went black. He felt Dennis lift him and pin him to the wall by his wrists. He'd apparently learned his lesson about leaving Keith's hands free.

Dennis's twisted face came back into focus. He waited. Keith knew that he wanted him to struggle, so he didn't.

"Tough old man. But the world is moving on. You're an antique. You're obsolete. You're the old model monster, and there's not room for both of us."

Dennis paused. Keith didn't reply. So Dennis continued. "But like I said, I'm not going to kill you yet. First, I'm going to take everything you have that's good and make it bad. Everything you haven't managed to ruin yourself, I'm going to ruin. Now that doesn't leave much to work with," Dennis laughed, "but I've done what I could. I just paid a visit to your brother."

Finally Keith struggled. He could ignore threats to himself, but Dennis had known where to strike. He yanked at the cold hands that clamped his wrists to the wall. He let his legs go loose and tried to drop from Dennis's grip. Dennis had gotten so strong. Panting, Keith finally stopped.

Dennis said, "The first thing you'll want to do is go over there and finish them off. Because I left them alive. So Roy and Sheila are gonna turn soon. And they won't be like me. They'll be mindless, stinking, slobbering beasts."

Keith ground his teeth, but didn't move. Dennis shrugged. "See, I'm unique. It's a lonely existence. So tonight I'm going to make a companion. I'm going to turn Jessica."

Keith snapped again, thrashing and bellowing. "I'll kill you. I swear to God and the Devil that I will hunt you down and gut you."

"Shhh. Hush. We both know that's not gonna happen. But you can sure give it a shot, tough guy. After you take care of Roy and Sheila, you'd better find me before sunrise, because that's when I make Jessica the second true vampire."

Dennis pulled Keith back and slammed him into the wall. Slowly at first. Casually. As if to show him how easy it was.

But then harder and harder, until Keith felt his back smash through the sheetrock and bounce between exposed studs. He was nearly unconscious when Dennis dropped him. He could only just make out Dennis's face and the fangs that seemed to have grown with his excitement.

"But if you find me," Dennis said, "I'm just gonna make you watch as I turn her, and then I'm gonna feed you to her."

Dennis stood. He retracted his fangs. He turned to leave, and as he walked out the front door, he said, "But you do as your conscious tells you."

Keith got shakily to his feet. In his bedroom, he pulled his boots on. He took a small revolver from his night stand and slid it into the top of his right boot. He took his Ruger .45 semi-automatic from the top of his closet and stuck it in the back of his jeans.

As thoughts entered his brain, he pushed them away; he focused on his anger.

Down in the living room he picked up his gore-covered pocketknife. He wiped it on the leg of his jeans. Not much of the mess came away but he folded it and slipped it into his pocket. He took his hatchet and hunting knife from the hall closet and clipped them to his belt. He grabbed his hat and his shotgun and started out the door.

He paused and turned back, looking around the living room. Irene's living room.

He pushed his thoughts away, put his hat on his head, and walked out the door.

In his truck, Keith tore down the short stretch of dirt road to Roy's house. Two of his hounds barked and bounced excitedly in the back. They always picked up Keith's mood.

Roy's house loomed close when something hit Keith's door hard enough to knock the truck up off its driver's-side tires for a moment. Keith turned his head away from the road and saw Dennis's fanged face smiling at him from only inches away. Latched onto the side of the moving truck, Dennis ripped Keith's door off and tossed it into the night. Then he did the same to Keith.

When Keith rolled to a stop in the ditch, Dennis was standing over him. "Hurry, Keith. Sheila's turned."

Keith's dogs jumped from the back of the truck and ran at the pair, but Dennis sprinted away. The dogs turned to follow until Keith called them back.

The truck choked and stalled and Keith got his shotgun out of it before running up to Roy's house. The dogs ran at his heels.

"Stay."

They whimpered but didn't follow him up and into the dark house.

The front door lay in splintered chunks. Keith walked carefully through the doorway with his shotgun to his shoulder. Glass crunched under his boot heels. There was no point in being quiet anyway.

He walked slowly across the foyer and until he could see down the short hallway to the kitchen. The kitchen light was on, and there, framed in the doorway, stood Sheila and Roy. Sheila had Roy grasped in a bear hug, her face buried in his neck. As Keith stepped into the hallway, she saw him and shrieked but still held Roy to her chest.

Keith slung the shotgun and drew his .45. Sheila didn't even seem to recognize what he was doing. She stared at him, fangs bared, as he aimed and fired.

Her head snapped back, its contents hitting the far wall, and she dropped to the floor. Roy turned to Keith and clutched his throat. Blood poured from around his fingers and from his mouth. Silent, he dropped.

Keith sat on the kitchen floor, Roy's head in his lap. Roy clutched at Keith at first, but soon he faded.

"You were such a sweet kid. Always wanting to do whatever I did. In some ways you're still that kid. But you should have stopped following me. I should have stopped letting you.

"I don't think you were cut out for this life. It seems like out here you can work hard, take care of your family, go to church every Sunday, and there's still some decision to be made that'll make you question the sort of man you are. You talked about our burden of sin, but what did you ever know about it? I figured I already knew the sort of man I was, so I was always willing to take on your share. Now I guess I will again. After Irene died, you and Sheila and Jessica managed to keep that small part of me that was still human alive. But I think this is too much, Roy."

Roy's hand had fallen away from his throat. Blood no longer spurted out, but leaked out slowly.

"I can do this. I can keep you from becoming one of them. But a man can only take on so much sin before losing himself. I think this is going to be it."

Keith stood and Roy's head thumped on the floor.

"But I suppose I deserve it. Goodbye, Roy."

Keith shouted for Jessica. He searched the house but he knew he wouldn't find her. Keith didn't consider Dennis at all trustworthy on average, but when it came to taking his revenge he'd been honest up to that point. Dennis had taken her, and Keith would have to find her–quickly.

Keith walked out of the kitchen door to Roy's tool shed. He grabbed the gas can from beside the lawnmower.

Walking back, he noticed a pinprick of light beaming out from the house. He was confused for a moment. Then he realized that the bullet he'd shot Sheila with had gone through her skull and then straight through the wall.

Back in the house, Keith splashed gasoline all around the first floor, ending in the kitchen. He drenched the corpses of his brother and sister-in-law, then realized he had no matches. He knew there'd be some in the junk drawer, but the fumes were making him sick to his stomach by the time he found them.

When he flicked a match through the door, the house erupted immediately.

Keith stood and watched it burn. But in his head he was damning himself. In his head, he was knocking at Dennis's trailer door.

"What the Hell do you want?" Dennis had asked.

"I want to buy some morphine."

Dennis stuck his head out the door and looked around. "Is this some kind of joke?"

Keith didn't respond.

"No, you don't make jokes, do you? Why do you want morphine?"

"Why do you care?"

Dennis nodded. "I guess I don't." He stepped aside and with a sweep of his arm said, "Welcome to my abode."

"Just bring it out."

Dennis shrugged. "Whatever."

He closed the door. A minute later, he opened it.

"You're lucky. I don't usually have morphine, but I just traded some off a vet."

"A veteran?"

"A veterinarian."

"This is for animals?"

"It's all the same."

"How much?"

Dennis smiled.

At the hospital, Keith had sat the vial of morphine and the hypodermic needle on Irene's tray.

"He said that's enough?" she asked.

"I asked him for enough for ten times. I figure that even with your tolerance, that's enough."

"You don't think he cheated you?"

Keith raised an eyebrow.

"No, I suppose he didn't," she said.

Irene picked up the needle and tried to stick it into the vial. Her hands shook too badly. Keith watched until she jabbed herself in the thumb and dropped the vial.

"Here," he said. He drew all the morphine up into the syringe. Irene tried to take it from him, but he shook his head and stuck the needle into the IV.

"I'm sorry," she said. "I love you."

"I love you too."

Eventually she said, "I'm ready."

Keith pressed the plunger. Irene's breathing slowed immediately. He pulled her into his arms and held her until she died.

The kitchen door exploded out. Flames erupted from the opening as something tumbled down the short flight of stairs. It dragged itself along the ground, away from the burning house. The flames covering its body began to go out. It was Roy.

Keith watched him for a moment, then walked over. Roy didn't react, didn't acknowledge Keith's presence. He continued to crawl away. His skin was a mottled blend of wet red and flaky black. He wouldn't have wanted to be a vampire. So with his hatchet, Keith took another burden upon himself.

He drug Roy's body back up the short set of concrete stairs. He instinctively held his breath as he felt the heat from the fire. He pushed Roy back inside the door, then tossed Roy's head in after the body.

Keith watched the house burn for another few minutes. As it started to collapse, he took his dogs and followed them into the night.

CHAPTER 17

Dennis slipped quietly into the barn. At the far end, his herd had mostly settled in for the night. The addition of Sheriff Wheeler had caused some commotion, but soon they sank back into their own personal misery. Someone was whimpering. It sounded like Patty, with the smashed face and the broken bones. He felt a bit bad for her, but he was surprised that he didn't feel worse. They'd been pretty friendly before. But he was of a different species now, a more advanced species. He felt no real moral bonds to her. He was predator; she was prey. He didn't want her to suffer though. Keith would be there soon, and once he finished with him he'd end her suffering.

He turned his ears up to the loft overhead, heard frustrated grunts and weight shifting. Sounded like Jessica was trying to get out of her ropes. He walked further into the barn, then turned and jumped up to the loft.

Squatted in her nightshirt, Jessica looked at him like a guilty animal, then set her jaw in that Harris way.

"Cut that out, now," Dennis said. "I left them loose so they wouldn't hurt. You don't want me to tie you up like I did them down there." He gestured towards the milking stalls at the other end of the barn.

"What in the Hell is wrong with you?"

He ignored the question and came forward with his offering. "I thought you might be thirsty. I snagged you a beer." He opened it and tried to hold it to her mouth, but she turned away, whipping her hair over his hands. He wasn't hungry, but he still struggled. He'd have to control himself very carefully when the time came to turn her. If the smell of her hair alone excited him, the taste of her blood would be even worse.

He said, "Enjoy it while you can. Soon you'll only drink blood."

"What did you do to my parents?"

"They're fine." He didn't want to lie to her. He didn't mind lying that much, but he didn't feel it was the right way to start a relationship that could last for a very, very long time. But he thought it would be more than she could handle right then. She'd understand after she changed. She'd see that they'd been only cattle. "I wouldn't hurt your family."

"Well, my family will hurt you. My uncle Keith will hunt you down. You have got to be the single dumbest asshole I've ever known. Do you know what he's gonna do to you, Dennis? Do you? I've already been trying to keep him from killing you."

That respect. Keith was nothing but a mean redneck, and everyone gave him that respect. But he'd break him down right in front of her. He'd show her that it was all show, that behind the front Keith put up hid a weak, scared man. Once he'd done that, he'd finally get the respect he deserved. "I know what your uncle is gonna do. He's gonna follow the trail I left his dogs and come right through that door. But he won't save you. I'll save you."

Jessica scoffed and almost spoke, but Dennis wasn't going to let her scorn him anymore. "I'll save you from a boring, normal life, and I'll save you from him.

"From who?" He could see real confusion on her face, but he was going to straighten her out.

"See this?" Dennis extended his arm.

"Your bad arm. It works."

"You didn't say anything earlier."

"It wasn't my first concern."

"You know how it got bad?"

"I heard rumors."

"You heard rumors that your uncle did it?"

"Yeah. Rumors."

"He's not the man you think he is. I helped him–"

Jessica barked out a laugh. "How could you ever help him?"

"I helped him! And in return he crippled me. Wrecked my shoulder so bad that the broken bones cut up all the nerves and they never healed. He's not the man you think. He's a lunatic. You want to know how I helped him?"

"Yeah, sure." Jessica rolled her eyes.

"I sold him morphine."

"Oh yeah?"

"Yeah. About a day before his wife died of a morphine overdose. Equipment malfunction."

And he had her attention. "That's a lie."

"You ever wonder why he didn't go after the hospital or the IV manufacturer? Why he signed all their papers so quickly? Because then they would have had their own investigators look into it."

Then the disbelief was back in her face. "He didn't sue them because he didn't want anything from them. I don't believe for a second that he bought anything from you. He never would have killed Irene. He might as well kill himself. She was everything to him."

"You can't get into his head and understand him. Nothing's beyond a psycho like that." Dennis smiled. "Well, nothing except me. I'm well beyond him now." He snarled and let all his fangs show. She cringed, but not enough. He punched the wall, putting a deep dent in the steel. She wasn't sneering anymore.

"What are you?" she asked. "A vampire?"

"I think so. That's the only thing that makes sense. Soon, you'll be one too, and this whole county will be ours. You can't imagine what it's like. The power. Imagine being able to do anything you want. Imagine being so strong that you can take anything you want. You had a taste for meth." He smiled, and she looked down. "Imagine tweaking all the time, the world moving in slow motion around you. I'm going to give that to you."

"Why me?" she asked.

Dennis let his fangs retract some and knelt beside her. "I've liked you for a long time, but you were Brandon's girl."

"We fooled around a couple of times when I was high. I was not his girl."

"Well, he wanted you to be, and you could've done worse. Anyway, you're not like the rest of these country bumpkins. You're tough and smart and pretty, and soon you'll be more powerful than you can imagine." He ran a claw along her strong jaw line.

She jerked her head away and glared at him. "And I'm Keith's."

"See, I said you were smart. And you're Keith's. And once I take you away from him, he'll have nothing."

Jessica's tough expression held for a moment, then melted. "What you said about my parents... What do you mean 'he'll have nothing?'"

The discussion was over anyway. He picked up a short length of thick rope and wrapped it around her head. She clamped her mouth shut, but he worked the coarse fibers across her lips until she had to relent to the gag.

"I need to go take care of a few things. I know you're upset right now, but I promise you, once I turn you, you'll get perspective. None of these heifers matter a bit."

Dennis turned and stepped over the edge of the loft.

CHAPTER 18

As Keith jogged behind his dogs through the pastures, he thought about how he'd gotten into this mess. He'd never thought much of it before, when Dennis was a worthless crippled junky. But Keith had drawn the anger of this monster on himself.

He'd been leaning on his truck outside Dennis's trailer when Dennis pulled up in his old beater car. Keith remembered Dennis hesitating for a moment, but then stepping out with a case of beer.

"Hey, Keith. What's going on?"

Hidden beneath Keith's crossed arms was his .45, and he pistol-whipped Dennis in the face with it.

Dennis dropped to the dirt, holding his face and screaming. He had one hand on his shattered cheekbone and one hand on the ground. Keith put his boot heel on that hand, and his gun to Dennis's head.

"My niece was found with drugs. If you ever sell her drugs again, you'll die."

"I never sold Jessica drugs. Jessica is Brandon's girl."

"Brandon's girl?"

"I mean, they don't do anything, just hang out–"

"Shut up. I know you're the leader. If anyone sells Jessica drugs again, I'll kill you."

Brandon opened the door, rubbing his eyes as if he'd just woken up. Keith pointed the gun in his direction. Brandon slammed the door.

"I never done shit to you," Dennis said. "I didn't sell to Jessica. I kept quiet about you buying morphine off me, even after your wife ODed."

"What?"

"I... I did you a favor, man. Your wife... I did you a favor!"

His old tunnel vision came back. He couldn't even say why exactly because Dennis was right. But things closed in on him, went dark on him, like they had back before Irene. He had Dennis's hand pinned with one boot heel. He stomped Dennis with the other. He stomped his shoulder again and again. He could feel things snapping. Distantly, he could hear Dennis screaming.

Then the trailer door opened again, and Brandon stood there with a shotgun.

Keith stared down his .45 at Brandon, but he stepped off of Dennis. Dennis curled up into a ball. Keith left him there crying in the dirt.

He supposed that if he looked back over his life, he could find a hundred such times where he'd damned himself. But that one seemed to have stuck.

Keith followed his dogs right up to the big dairy barn. Standing against the fence on either side of the barn, dairy cattle with swollen udders lowed piteously. Keith wondered that the neighbors hadn't heard it, then understood that

Dennis had probably already gotten the neighbors. Keith walked up to the big metal door. The dogs were ready to lead Keith inside, but he unleashed them.

"Home," he said. They whimpered and spun in circles.

"Home." They turned and ran. Keith readied his shotgun and slid the big door open just wide enough to slip inside.

Pointing the flashlight into the darkness, he saw nothing. He searched the wall for the light switch and flipped it on. The fluorescents popped to buzzing life.

At the other end of the barn, Dennis held Jessica against himself. He gripped the back of her head and pressed her face into his chest, and he smiled.

"Let her go, Dennis."

"No."

"She's got nothing to do with this. I'm the one you want. Let her go and take me." Keith heard a shuffling sound above him but couldn't look away from Dennis and Jessica.

"No, no, no. I've heard this before!" Dennis took on a John Wayne drawl and said, "Let that pretty little thing go and take me instead." Then in his normal voice, "You're not a goddamn hero!"

"So what do you want me to say?"

"I want you to beg."

"I'm begging you—"

"On your knees."

Keith dropped to his knees. They were weak anyway. He was weak. There was nothing he could do with her in Dennis's grasp. "I'm begging you."

The shuffling above got louder and bits of straw fell around him, but he couldn't take his eyes off of Dennis, even when Dennis looked up with a strange expression on his face.

"Come here," Dennis said. "Now."

But before Keith could get to his feet a rattlesnake rattle hit the concrete in front of him. He looked up and saw Jessica looking down at him from the loft above. She was gagged and had shaken the necklace over her dangling head.

Keith brought his shotgun to bear on Dennis but Dennis roared and threw Patty Seller aside while he dove in the opposite direction. Patty hit a metal post with a sickening thud and crumpled to the ground. Keith fired, but too late.

From one of the stalls, Dennis said, "I'm gonna start calling you Molasses Keith with a draw like that."

Dennis had jumped to the right. Keeping his shotgun to his shoulder, Keith edged slowly down the left side of the aisle.

"Hey, Keith, you know what makes even better eating than humans?"

With a shriek, a shriveled old vampire came careening out of a milking stall near the end of the aisle. Looking back over its shoulder, it moved like it was trying to put as much distance between itself and Dennis as it could. When it finally looked forward, Keith saw that it was old Logan. Logan slid to a stop, then shrieked again and launched himself through the air at Keith. Keith shot him like he was a clay and stepped aside. Logan's body slapped the concrete right beside him, white and thin limbed with a soft, loosely-fleshed torso. Before it could rise, Keith put the shotgun against the old man's head and blew it apart.

"Keith," someone said from his left. He recognized the voice and hurried forward, shotgun still at his shoulder.

"Bill, is that you?"

Sheriff Wheeler lay on his side on the concrete floor with his wrists and ankles hogtied behind him. He was battered and bloody, but still had a bit of the spark in his eye that annoyed Keith so much.

"You've gotta stop him," Wheeler said.

Keith glanced around. No Dennis. He knew that dropping his guard was dangerous, but between the two of them they could pin Dennis down. Keith sat his shotgun aside, pulled his pocketknife out and sawed at the rope binding Wheeler's limbs together.

"Keith!" Wheeler shouted.

Keith glanced over his shoulder just in time to see a clawed hand grab the back of his shirt. It wrenched him from the stall and threw him across the aisle, where he slammed into a metal gate before sliding to the concrete.

Dennis smiled as he walked towards Keith. Keith hurled his pocketknife at Dennis's face.

"Oh God!" Dennis screamed, gripping the knife in both hands, but he started laughing and held the knife out. He took his other hand away from his unmarked face. He'd caught the knife. "Fool me once—"

Keith whipped the hunting knife from his belt into Dennis's eye.

Dennis shrieked and grabbed the hunting knife in both hands, perfectly mimicking the movements he'd made a moment before in jest. With shaking hands he slowly pulled the hunting knife from his eye and dropped it aside.

Keith had made it to one knee and fumbled for the revolver in his boot before Dennis roared and leapt at him. Keith saw he didn't have the time and instead stood to meet him, quickly pulling the hatchet from his belt and slamming it into his gut. Dennis didn't pause, but backhanded Keith against the cage door.

Knocked on his ass, Keith had no choice but to fish the damned revolver from his boot. Just as Dennis closed in for the kill, Keith yanked the gun free and fired all five rounds into Dennis's chest, point blank.

Dennis fell face-first before Keith, clawing at the concrete, but Keith knew now that that wasn't the end of it. He tossed the revolver aside and scrambled to his knees, hatchet-in-hand.

But Dennis scurried away even faster. He made it to his feet, and after a few staggering steps, gained speed and leapt up into the loft.

Battered, bloody and already aching, Keith ran for the ladder to the loft. Slipping the hatchet into its belt-clip, he grabbed the rungs and began to climb. Jessica shouted, "Keith!" and he climbed faster.

He'd barely made it off the ground before Dennis flew over him, carrying Jessica. He landed with a crunch as the concrete beneath his shoes cracked. He set Jessica on her feet. He'd untied her mouth and feet up in the loft, but held a rope that bound her wrists behind her back.

"Keith, do you know what I want?"

Keith nodded. "Revenge."

"Can you blame me?"

"I can't."

"You're no hero, Keith."

"I never claimed to be."

"No, I suppose you didn't. But you strode in here jingle-jangling like you were going to settle some foolishness."

Keith noticed Sheriff Wheeler slowly creeping out of a stall behind Dennis with Keith's shotgun in his hands. He was shoeless and moved with cartoonish care. Keith's eyes snapped back to Dennis. "What do you want me to do?"

"I want you to tell Jessica how you killed her aunt."

Keith hesitated. Dennis reeled Jessica in on her rope and tilted her head to the side.

"Okay," he said to Dennis, then to Jessica, "You know Irene was very sick. She was suffering a lot. She asked me to help her—"

"Tell her that you murdered her," Dennis said.

"I murdered Irene."

Tears streamed down Jessica's cheeks.

"I'm sorry, Jessica. I didn't want to."

"It's not your fault," she said.

"Then whose fault is it?" Keith asked.

"No one's. Sometimes things happen and it's no one's fault."

Keith risked a glance at Sheriff Wheeler. He was trying to get to a position where he could take a shot without hitting Jessica. Keith knew that the closer he got, the more likely Dennis was to hear him. All he could think to do was keep talking.

"I don't know. I was supposed to protect her. Our whole marriage, I tried to shield her from the bad. But in the end, I killed her. In the end, I couldn't protect anybody. I destroy. Seems like that's all I can manage."

"You're here to protect me," Jessica said. "You're still a good man, even if you've made mistakes. We all make mistakes. I sure as Hell have. All we can do is try."

"How sweet," Dennis said. "It just—" And then Dennis's mouth filled with fangs and all his muscles went tense as he spun around. Keith didn't hear whatever alerted Dennis, but something had.

"Move, Jessica!" Keith said.

Jessica jumped to the end of the rope and Sheriff Wheeler blasted Dennis in the chest with the shotgun, sending him toppling over backwards. But Dennis immediately began to struggle for his feet. Sheriff Wheeler put the barrel of the gun to Dennis's head and pulled the trigger. It clicked on an empty chamber. Wheeler flipped the gun, holding it by the barrel, and smashed the stock down on Dennis's head as he rose. He swung again, but Dennis caught it.

"Get clear," Keith yelled to Wheeler. He'd pulled his .45 but couldn't get a clean shot. Wheeler yanked at the shotgun, trying to tear it from Dennis's grip. Dennis used the gun to pull Sheriff Wheeler in. He knocked the Sheriff out with one punch.

"Get out of here," Keith said to Jessica.

"What about you?"

"I have to kill him."

Dennis tossed the Sheriff aside with disturbing ease.

"Or at least slow him down. Go!"

The slap of Jessica's bare feet on concrete got Dennis's attention. Fully enraged, Dennis ran after her. Keith began shooting him center-mass. Black blood and gore exploded out of Dennis's back. Dennis didn't slow, but he did change directions.

Running through the bullets Dennis tackled Keith to his back, sending the gun spinning out of his hand. Dennis crawled up Keith's chest and pinned his arms with his hands.

"You thought this was a fight?" Dennis snarled. "This was me toying with you. How does it feel to be the one squirming in the dirt, your life in the hands of a merciless bastard?"

Dennis calmed himself. His face became more human. "Damn it, Keith. I've got a feeling this is going to be a boring existence. You're the toughest hombre out there, and look at what I've done to you. Say I'm really immortal. How am I going to entertain myself for the rest of eternity if you're the best the world has to offer?" Dennis smiled.

"Well, Jessica and I will probably manage to distract each other."

"We both know why you need to talk so big, little man. Just shut up and do what you're gonna do."

Dennis laughed. "Goddamn, the Devil made you mean. I hope some of that evil's in your blood."

Dennis pinned Keith's left arm with his knee, then slammed a palm into that shoulder. It snapped as easily as if Dennis had hit it with a sledge hammer. Keith gritted his teeth as Dennis ground the broken shoulder into the concrete.

"Now we're even," Dennis said. "Now you're just a meal." He pressed Keith's head back with both hands and bit into his neck.

The draining of his blood was one of the strangest sensations he'd ever felt, and Keith wrapped the fingers of his right hand in Dennis's hair and pulled. Dennis was far too strong for this to have any effect. In fact, he seemed to enjoy it.

With his head pressed back, Keith watched Jessica sneak back into the barn, her arms still tied behind her back. He said, "No," but Jessica kept coming. Dennis seemed to think Keith was begging, and began to feed even more greedily.

Jessica kicked the .45 Ruger. Keith reached out and snatched it up with his good hand.

"Dennis!" Jessica yelled.

"Wha–?" Dennis looked up, dazed and blood drunk, and Keith smashed the .45 through his fangs and pulled the trigger three times. Dennis fell over backwards, bent at the knees. His jaws snapped reflexively at the air.

As Keith awkwardly tipped Dennis off of him with his good arm, Jessica knelt beside him. "Are you okay?" she asked.

"No."

Keith rose to his knees, took the hatchet from his belt and hacked Dennis's head off. He tossed the head across the barn, as far from the body as he could get it, just to be sure.

Sweat ran down Keith's face and blood ran from his neck. The exertion made his head swoon even worse and the world began to pulse black around the edges and then blur. His blood roared in his ears as he sat back onto the concrete and reached for the .45. He put it against his temple.

"Keith!" Jessica shouted.

He pulled the trigger, but nothing happened. Forcing his eyes to focus, he looked at the gun. The slide was still kicked back. He'd used the last bullet on Dennis.

"Damn it!" he shouted as he threw the gun across the barn.

Jessica knelt and examined his neck. "You can make it, Keith. Just put some pressure on it. They can fix this."

"He bit me. I'm becoming one of them."

Sheriff Wheeler staggered over to them and untied Jessica's hands.

"You did it, Keith. That was amazing."

Keith could tell that he was trying to put the past behind them, but it didn't matter. Keith thrust his hatchet at the Sheriff. "I'm turning. I need you to finish me off."

"What? No. I can't. I'm a man of the law."

"You can't let me become one of them. It ain't right."

"I've never killed anyone. I'm a man of the–"

"Goddamn it, Bill! You can't do this to me."

"I'm sorry."

The hatchet disappeared from Keith's outstretched hand. It took a moment for him to understand that Jessica had taken it, not Wheeler. The Sheriff reached for the hatchet, but she raised it menacingly.

"Back off," she said. "Way back."

Wheeler turned around and walked away. He was a coward, but Keith could at least thank him for that. He could in good conscience say he didn't know how Keith had died.

When Wheeler was gone, Keith said, "I can't ask you to do this."

"You don't have to. You came here prepared to do the same for me."

Keith nodded. He got to his knees and leaned forward, exposing the nape of his neck. Then Jessica wrapped her arms around him, almost knocking him over. She said, "Do you think I'll be judged for this, after I die?"

Keith had to think a moment. He felt himself fading, but she deserved an answer. He looked back over his own life now that it was over. He said, "It's easy to do the right thing when it feels good. But if you can do the right thing even when it kills you inside, God will know. Maybe you can barely look at yourself in the mirror anymore, but He knows."

"Say hello to Irene for me," Jessica said. She raised the hatchet as he closed his eyes.

CHAPTER 19

Covered in blood and wearing an oversized Looney Tunes t-shirt, Jessica walked out across the dark pasture. She gripped the gory hatchet in one hand and her rattlesnake necklace in the other. She felt Wheeler watching her go. He didn't say anything. It didn't matter. She wouldn't have responded.

She stood before her house. No one had called the fire department. No one had noticed. Nothing remained but ashes and cinders. And like her house, her life was gone. Her memories were ashes of people who no longer existed.

Jessica stood perfectly still. There was nothing left to motivate her to action. She had no reason to move. She would stand there until the ground swallowed her and the house and all the ashes of her life.

But a vampire shrieked in the distance. Then another, and another. Jessica slipped her necklace on, to protect herself from venomous creatures. She gripped her hatchet tighter. She set her jaw, turned her back on her lost home, and walked into the night.

ABOUT THE AUTHOR

Alan Ryker (born 1979) writes good fight scenes because he studies Muay Thai boxing, though not as often as his coach would like. He lives with his wife in Overland Park, a suburb of Kansas City, where he writes both dark and literary fiction, and tests the boundaries of each. He has previously published short fiction in a number of print anthologies and magazines.

Check out his many adventures at his blog, Pulling Teeth at www.alanryker.com. Enjoy his most mundane thoughts by following him on twitter: @alanryker. And contact him at alanjryker@gmail.com.

CPSIA information can be obtained at www.ICGtesting.com
Printed in the USA
LVOW090756051211

257858LV00001B/32/P